# THE GIFT

# The Gift
*Rick Incorvia*

# The Gift
*Rick Incorvia*

# Chapter 1 - Gift or Curse

When Tim's 5 a.m. alarm buzzed softly, he expected the day to be like every other. He'd have a three-mile run, a healthy breakfast and a long hot shower before he headed in to work.

When the phone rang at 5:05, he knew something was wrong. His staff knew not to bother him before 8. That was his "private time."

"Hello, Tim speaking."

The line was silent long enough for him to consider hanging up. "Tim Kerbric?" a deep voice asked.

"Who wants to know?" Tim replied with a bit of attitude.

"This is Sergeant Jenkins at the Beacon City police department. I'm afraid we have some bad news." Again silence, as if he was waiting for Tim to ask a question. Tim waited patiently. "There's been an accident. Well, more like an incident."

Okay, now he had Tim's attention. "Well, are you going to tell me or make me guess?" Tim glowered as if the voice on the other end could see how irritated he was. "I'm sorry, Mr. Kerbric. I understand you were good friends with Hoyt Pendleton. May I ask when was the last time you saw him?"

"You certainly can ask, but you're not getting another word out of me until you tell me what the hell this is all about. You do know it's 5 o'clock in the morning." Tim hesitated, tightening his grip on the phone and wrinkling up his forehead. *Why won't this cop tell me what's up with Hoyt?* He was getting angrier by the moment. This was his best friend they were talking about. "Was he in an accident? Is he in some kind of trouble?"

"Actually, Mr. Kerbric, we were hoping he was with you. We got a call from his wife last night. She says a couple of professionals broke into the house and roughed her up a bit.

"Lisa? Lisa is hurt?" A surge of desperation rose in Tim's throat.

"She's fine. She says he might be with you. Something about Thursday night cards with the boys. She says you all play cards every Thursday. What time did Hoyt leave your place last night?"

"What? Wait," Tim stammered. "I haven't seen Hoyt in months."

The line remained silent.

"Said they were looking for something they called 'The Gift.' Any idea what they meant by 'The Gift'?"

"What? No!" None of this was making any sense. There was more to this story than he was hearing. After a long moment of silence, Tim demanded, "Who is this?"

The officer muttered slowly, "Like I said, I am Sergeant Jenkins. I can't tell you any more over the phone, Mr. Kerbric, but I think it would be in your best interest to come to the station."

Tim hung up the phone. He tried to wipe the sleep from his face. He dragged his hands through his hair a few times and slipped yesterday's shirt over his head. He pulled a pair of blue jeans from his laundry basket and clumsily hopped on one foot, trying to slip the second foot into the pants leg. By the time he slipped his sockless feet into his black loafers his mind began to catch up with what he'd just heard. *It sounds like someone broke into Hoyt and Lisa's house and Hoyt is still missing.* He wondered if this had been just another fight over Hoyt's obsessive work ethic.

Tim suddenly remembered a call he'd gotten from Hoyt a few days ago. He had sounded out of breath and heavily caffeinated. "I did it, Tim," Hoyt puffed, "I fuckin' did it." Assuming that Hoyt had finally told Lisa he wanted a divorce, Tim had settled in for one of Hoyt's rants. "It's all about the blood flow. Who knew? I'll tell you who knew . . . I knew, that's who." Just out of the shower, Tim had responded robotically. "Of course you did, Hoyt. You're the smartest guy I know."

Tim had been about to tell Hoyt he'd call him back when Hoyt interrupted. "It's all about basic vitamins, minerals and properly timed frequencies." The guy was uninterruptible. "You have to come over!" Tim could barely hear Hoyt over the treadmill. *That damn treadmill.* Hoyt spent hours on that treadmill every day. He said it helped him think. Hoyt didn't give Tim time to answer. "I gotta go. Call me tomorrow. You're gonna love this."

On the way to the police station, Tim played the conversation over and over in his head. Thinking back, he began to realize that Hoyt had been especially intense lately. He knew Hoyt wasn't the cheating type. The more he thought about the phone call, he figured the lie about Thursday night cards was an excuse to spend time at the lab. Time to work on some kind of breakthrough.

And that got him thinking about another phone conversation, weeks earlier. Hoyt had called him. He'd confided that he was deep into mineral enhancements and absorption rates, which put him on the brink of developing a better mental awareness product. It was sure to put him into the big leagues, he'd insisted. It was hush-hush but was apparently a mix between science and technology. But just as he'd started to tell Tim about his breakthroughs, he'd stopped abruptly. Softly, almost in a whisper, he'd said he couldn't really talk about it yet.

At the station, two cops watched silently as Tim's eyes met Lisa's for the first time. "Oh, my God Lisa! What happened?"

Lisa was breathing hard, her eyes red. She couldn't keep her hands still. "Do you know where he is? I can't find him. I think he's in trouble." Tim hugged her and did his best to calm her.

The police quickly steered them apart into two separate interrogation rooms. "What am I doing in here?" Tim snapped. "Am I a suspect?"

Sergeant Jenkins didn't introduce himself, but Tim recognized him from his deep voice. "A suspect for what? Do you know what happened to Hoyt?" Tim tightened his lips and went silent for a moment. This was the voice from 5:05 a.m., just as annoying in person.

"Do I need my lawyer?"

The officer smiled and chuckled, "No, Mr. Kerbric, I just had to find a quiet place to talk. The station has been a zoo all night, like someone is passing out crazy pills." A fellow cop poked his head in and asked if he could see the sergeant for a minute. Jenkins shot the intruder the "Can't you see I'm busy" look and then slowly proceeded to stand as if it pained him to be on his feet. He was awkwardly tall and sported the typical police belly, no doubt from too much paperwork and too many donuts.

He left Tim alone in the room for nearly twenty minutes. When he finally came back he repeated his crazy pills line from earlier. When Tim had gotten Jenkins' call at 5:05 this morning, he had been aggravated. Now, he was all the way to pissed off. Sergeant Jenkins started talking again. "Look, we're hoping you have something that might help us find Hank."

"His name is Hoyt," snapped Tim, irritated that the officer was either not taking this seriously or just couldn't be bothered. Tim knew Hoyt had borrowed a large amount of "hard money" from some pretty shady guys to develop his "Enhancements" or whatever he was working on. But he had no intention of giving up this information before hearing everything that Lisa had to say.

* * *

Lisa was in the next room struggling through a similar experience. Two officers were in the unusually warm room with her. Officer Melbern was a pudgy older man, stuffed into a cheap wool suit. His five-foot three-inch fireplug of a body was circling the table like a shark. His breathing was labored and he took turns wiping the sweat from his right brow, then his left. Rubbing his palms onto the seat of his pants, he started his questioning. "When did you last see your husband?" When Lisa took too long to answer, he fired another question at her. "What were you two fighting about?"

Lisa backed up her head and blinked her eyes until they were wide open. "Don't even think about accusing me. I'm the one that called you."

Officer Anita Cleveland was a thin, fit woman in her mid-forties. The two officers looked at each other for just a moment and Officer Cleveland spoke up in a soft but firm voice. "These are standard questions that we have to ask the spouse. If not now, it always comes up later. Best if you just answer the questions."

Lisa sat up straight in her chair. "I don't like his attitude . . . Or the tone in his voice."

When Lisa calmed down, she told the officers that Hoyt had been missing for two days. "It wasn't unusual lately for him to spend the night at the lab. Yes, we'd been arguing some recently and I figured he was spending another night at the lab, obsessing over his latest discovery."

Officer Melbern jumped all over her response. "Another night? How often does your husband stay out all night?"

Lisa inhaled, ready for a heated response, but then recovered, closing her eyes and slowly letting her breath out through her nose.

Officer Cleveland, who up to now had mostly listened silently, started to jot down notes. This got Lisa nervous again. She sat back in her chair and folded her arms. After ten seconds of silence, Officer Cleveland spoke. Her voice was soft, reassuring. "Help us find him." Officer Melbern was standing between his partner and the one-way mirror, hands on his hips. Armpit sweat stained his jacket. Lisa had to close her eyes to stop taking in more details of this human train wreck. She struggled to collect her thoughts.

"I left him a message at the lab last night. It was about 10. I told him if he didn't come home, I was packing his stuff and putting it at the curb." Melbern and Cleveland listened without comment. "I must have fallen asleep around midnight. Later that night, I heard the door open and I figuring it was Hoyt trying to sneak in all quiet. I prepared myself for what you would call a little domestic quarrel" she said throwing a smug look at officer Melbern. "Then suddenly something bashed me on the head. I must have blacked out. When I started to come to, I could hear that someone was rummaging through every drawer in the house. And then I remember a guy yelling 'C'mon, let's go.' That's when somebody—it must have been a second guy—grabbed me by my hair. I couldn't see him, but he whispered in my ear, 'Where is "The Gift"?' I was too stunned and too scared to talk and that's when he hit me. It was a cell phone, I think." She instinctively touched the gash over her right eye, indicating that it was the second of the two gashes she'd gotten. The officers who showed up to the scene had cleaned her up and put butterfly bandages over her wounds before taking her to the station.

"When was the last time you saw your husband?"

Lisa snapped, "I told you. Two days ago."

The annoying cop continued his harassing tone. "And remind me: what were you fighting about?"

Lisa flipped him a subtle middle finger and said, "Take me home." She could see the two were looking at each other and thinking: *domestic issue.*

As they left the interrogation room Officer Cleveland suggested that Lisa check into the hospital. Lisa insisted on waiting for Tim and sat, arms folded, across from Officer Cleveland's desk. Ten agonizing minutes passed.

\* \* \*

Tim walked around the corner, hoping Lisa was still at the station. Officer Cleveland stood to greet him. She asked if he would be willing to swing past the hospital with Lisa to have her checked over. Tim nodded his head, silently agreeing, and mumbled under his breath. "C'mon, let's get out of here."

Officer Melbern, who was one desk over, had to get his last words in. "Stick around. We may have more questions for you" Tim could tell these cops weren't even sure a crime had been committed. Just inside the exit doors, Tim and Lisa gave the right of way to two cops who were struggling with an angry and slurring man of enormous size.

Giving this trio a wide berth, Tim grabbed both of Lisa's arms to get her attention off the cops and back to him. "Have you been to the lab?" Tim winced as he studied her banged-up face.

"No, I haven't been to the lab." Lisa widened her bloodshot eyes and pointed to her face. "In case you haven't noticed, I am a victim and these guys are questioning me like I did something. I know Hoyt is in trouble. He hasn't answered his phone in two days." Lisa brought her voice down to a whisper. "What is 'The Gift'?"

Tim just shook his head. He looked dumbfounded. He remembered Hoyt's words from earlier in the week. *"I did it, Tim . . . I fuckin' did it."*

His expression must have changed enough for Lisa to notice. She raised her eyebrow. "What? You know something. Tell me!"

"He told me that he 'did it' but I wasn't really listening. I thought you two had a fight and he finally left."

Lisa pulled her head back like she always did before making a statement. "Wait, what? Why would you say that? We're doing fine." This didn't sound convincing. She looked to see if any of the roomful of cops had heard Tim say that. She whispered to him, "We fight, but then we make up. Sometimes, we make up all night long." He was pretty sure from her body language what that meant.

*Atta boy, Hoyt.* Tim knew he'd better keep that thought to himself.

He led Lisa outside so they could continue their conversation without being overheard.

Lisa started right back at Tim. "Tell me exactly what he said to you."

Tim walked a few steps and then stopped. "I don't remember exactly." He paused a moment. "He said, 'I fuckin' did it!'" Tim closed his eyes and mimed holding a phone to his left ear. "Wait; then he said something about vitamins and minerals. But he was way too excited for whatever it was to be about; a better vitamin C tablet or a new dissolvable capsule. It sounded like he'd made a big breakthrough. Shit, I should have listened to him. I should have come to the lab."

Tim and Caroline used to hang out with Hoyt and Lisa every weekend. About five years before, Caroline had been diagnosed with cancer—the bad kind, non-small-cell lung carcinoma. The next two years were tough, consumed with chemo, special diets and vitamins. Hoyt had Tim's wife on a barrage of immune system builders, but in the end, the cancer still won. Tim didn't blame Hoyt, but he was still mad at him for giving him hope. Tim had stopped believing in magic pills and had never quite been able to get so involved again with Hoyt's latest vitamin hype. Hoyt and Lisa had still tried to invite Tim to events, but Tim felt more and more like a third wheel and began burying himself in his work. And all that, he reflected guiltily, had kept him from paying much attention to Hoyt lately.

"I'm not going to the hospital," Lisa said. After insisting that Tim come back to the house with her, she began to shake her head back and forth ever so slightly. "All I did was bitch at him for working late. We would be fighting within thirty minutes of him coming home. He'd disappear into the workout room and run forever on that stupid treadmill."

"He has a treadmill at home, too?" Tim asked. "Oh, my God. Are you kidding me?"

"He puts on that damn hat with the headphones and runs for hours," she continued. "Then he showers and comes to bed looking for action. Honestly, sometimes I think he's in there watching porn."

Tim pulled at his bottom lip. "Do you know what he listens to?" he asked.

"He says Mozart. Says it helps him unwind. But last week, I think he was learning another language."

"Another language . . ." This left Tim speechless for a moment. "Why would you say that?"

Lisa was wringing her hands. "I thought he was cheating on me or listening to a dirty-talk 800 number. Why else would he suddenly be so sexual? One night last week, I thought he had someone in there with him. I heard him speaking Italian—I think it was Italian—and it was a conversation, not just repeating a few words, or some sentence he'd rehearsed. I got closer to the door and I could tell it was his voice, so I thought he was on the phone with someone. How could my husband know another language without me knowing? We've been married for twelve years. I finally knocked on the door and ask him who he was talking to. When he didn't answer me, I opened the door and peeked in. He was wearing his stupid stocking cap with headphones. When he saw me, he yanked a cord out of the cap. It was plugged into his cell phone."

"Wait, he was wearing a stocking cap with headphones?" Tim interrupted. "What, like big noise-canceling headphones? Or earbuds?"

"No, the headphones are built into the cap. He got them off the internet. Wouldn't stop talking about them. Are you going to let me finish?"

She waved off Tim's questions, indicating he should have a little patience. "I asked him who he was talking to. He said he wasn't talking to anyone and that I should respect his privacy when he was in his room. I asked him what language he was speaking, and he just told me he was developing apps for learning. He looked down at his phone and I could see that both of our voices were being recorded. He picked up the phone and clicked a few commands on the keypad. He was yelling, 'Now I have to start from the beginning.'"

"Lisa, is that cap still at your house?" She raised her shoulders and twisted her hands, palms up, to indicate she didn't know. "Obviously, you've tried to call him. Does his phone go to voicemail or just ring?" Tim was firing questions at Lisa faster than she could answer. He reached for his phone and tapped in the three-digit speed-dial to his office number. "Hi, Chris. Yeah. Uh-huh. Listen, I'm not going to make it in to work for the next few days. Can you tell people I'm on vacation? Make up something. Yes! Everything is fine. Oh, I just have some personal stuff to take care of. Okay. Uh-huh. See you Monday."

Tim had made the mental switch to investigator mode. He may have watched too many reruns of CSI but when he pulled up into the driveway, he expected to see cops bustling about gathering clues or at least the door taped off. "Have the police been here yet? Have they dusted for fingerprints?"

Lisa looked at him with one eye raised. "Really, Tim. Yes, they were here, but I was afraid to stay at the house and made them take me to the police station. It was the middle of the night!" Tim was puzzled and opened his mouth to ask another question, but Lisa interrupted.

"They said they would send a squad car to keep an eye on the house, but I don't think they're taking this seriously because nothing was stolen. The cops did come here once, almost a year ago, for that big fight we got into. It was stupid. I'm sure they think this is more of the same thing, like a domestic violence issue. They probably think we had a fight and I'm protecting him or something."

Tim had no comment. He waited, expecting to hear more.

"It's not . . . right?" Lisa tightened her lips and clenched her fists. Her eyes were like slits and her head moved slightly back and forth as if to say, "How dare you?" Tim wished he could take back the question.

Lisa fumbled with the key. Her hands were shaking. Tim put his hands over hers and eased the key from her. Push, twist and slowly open. He planned to go straight to Hoyt's combined study and workout room but stopped to study the scene just inside the house. A single dining room chair was knocked over. All the knickknacks from the fireplace mantel were scattered, and shattered, across the tile floor. Kitchen drawers hung open and a small potted plant lay dumped into the sink. A long wooden coffee table, snapped in half, lay in a V shape as if someone very large had landed on it. Tim followed the mess into his friends' bedroom. "Wow, they tore up your bedroom."

"Yes, and my office."

"Did they get to his office?" Tim blurted.

Lisa reminded him that she had been in and out of consciousness while the intruders were in the house. "Something spooked them. I don't know how long I was out. But they broke my Noreen coffee table on their way out. When I woke up the second time, they were gone. I sat in front of the door, to be sure they couldn't sneak back in, and I dialed 911. A cop was here in ten minutes, but the guys were long gone. He helped me clean up my face and I asked him to take me to the station to make an official statement. I was afraid to drive there myself." She looked away a few seconds. "But I was more afraid to stay here in case they came back."

Lisa followed Tim to Hoyt's office. The door was open. Lisa hesitated. "This door is never left open." Tim entered, anticipating a disaster like he'd found elsewhere in the house. To his surprise, everything was in order. He was pretty sure no one had made it to Hoyt's office. He scanned the room, seeing plenty of confirmation of what he already knew, which was that Hoyt had a place for everything. On the desk was a note pad with yesterday's date. Below the date was a numbered list. Hoyt numbered everything.

1. Transfer funds

2. Gun

3. Call Tim

Tim picked up the list and showed it to Lisa. The pad of thin, lined paper drooped in his hand as he scanned the room. A hamper near the door overflowed with smelly workout clothes. In the immaculately organized room, it stood out like a sore thumb. Lying on top of the clothes was the stocking cap. Hoyt's phone was still attached.

Tim looked at Lisa and then studied the cap. He eased it over his tightly cropped head and adjusted it so the built-in circular headphones were right over his ears. He flipped the phone over as if it might have a secret button to push. He looked at Lisa for a nod of approval and pushed the "power on" button. He was discouraged to see the lock screen pop up. He turned the phone so Lisa could see the screen. "Of course, Hoyt has a secret code," he said.

"It's 1397."

"Hoyt told you his code?" Tim said, incredulous.

"Of course not. I've been trying to get it from him for the last two months. Something is weird with him. He is so distant and then so loving." Then she registered Tim's puzzled look. "It's the four corners of the pad. I saw him do it last week."

Tim tapped the pad's four corners, 1397. The phone opened to a recording. When Tim pressed the "play" icon, Hoyt's voice was making audio notes, recapping his latest thoughts from the night's work.

"Memory retention and cognitive learning is increased exponentially if you properly prepare to receive knowledge, properly receive knowledge and then lock it in. I believe our brain was designed to retain almost everything we experience with our five senses. I believe that I have uncovered the secret to audible learning with nearly 100 percent retention."

Lisa was all of five-foot-three and on her tip toes, ear to ear with six-foot-two Tim, trying to hear what her missing husband was saying. "I can't hear!" Tim shushed her with a wave of his hand. Lisa responded with a pissed-off glare and stuck her ear back against his.

"June 30th, 2016 notes. Retention is multiplied when we maintain extremely high levels of some basic vitamins and minerals like ascorbic acid, choline bitartrate, resveratrol, blah, blah, blah." Hoyt was famous for using "blah, blah, blah" when he felt he was carrying on about too much detail. "And . . . and . . . here's the surprise kicker." On the recording, Hoyt paused for effect. "You must maintain a heart rate of at least 120 beats per minute or higher." He laughed. "No one has figured that out till now. I have recently introduced two hundred fifty milligrams of N-acetyl-cysteine, ten milligrams of pyrroloquinoline quinone and one hundred milligrams of high potency CoQ10 and have been able to run for much longer periods, maintaining a heart rate of 120 to 135 beats per minute for nearly two hours."

Tim paused the recording. "I think we found the 'gift' they're after."

Lisa shook her head as she looked at Tim, as if she couldn't take him seriously with the silly cap on his head. He pushed "play" again. Lisa yanked the speaker plug from the phone and Hoyt's voice came loud and clear directly from the phone, easy for them both to hear. Lisa looked at Tim, a smug twist to her lips. "Take off the hat, dumbass."

Hoyt's voice continued: "The initial challenge with learning while the heart rate is over 120 bpm was that you're moving. Reading while running is not easy, so . . ." More hesitation and the sound of papers rustling. "So I dipped back into some old subliminal research from the 1970s; a Dr. Zemoremi claimed that certain high-pitched tones prepare the brain to accept audible information and that a specific low tone locks the information into long-term memory. Of course, everyone thought the doc was crazy and his results were weak because he didn't add nutrition into the mix—or the high heart rate. But using his research from a forty-five-year old book, I have been able to dial in the optimal subliminal high tone that opens the brain to learning." After another moment of silence, Hoyt began to speak again. The background noise was different, and Hoyt was obviously recording from somewhere much quieter. "Today is September 20th, 2016. I am amused by my old recordings. I have come so far in the last few months. I can barely contain myself. I have to show this to someone. And I am just about to –"

The recording went silent, except for a distinct rustling that must have been Hoyt taking off the cap. Lisa stared at Tim as if to echo his unspoken question: *Is that it? Is it over?* After what seemed like endless silence, but actually must have been less than a minute, the recording continued. Hoyt spoke in a whisper. "I think someone is in the house." Tim could hear faint noises over Hoyt's shuffling and the movement of his phone. "Shit. Someone *is* in the house." The recording went silent again, for a long time. Tim took the opportunity to turn the volume all the way up. He clearly heard Hoyt open his office door. Lisa caught his eye and nodded; she'd heard it too. After another twenty seconds of background noise, a distant voice faintly but clearly called, "Hoyt, is that you?" Lisa's mouth fell open. She was listening to her own voice from last night. Hoyt's recorded voice softly whispered, "Shit." A bang and clatter meant he must have dropped the phone. Footsteps raced away down the hall, followed by a scuffle and a big thud.

"Oh, my God!" Lisa said. "Hoyt was home last night when those guys came in. They took him!" They both stared at the phone. *Is there more?* A final voice, indistinctly, said, "C'mon, let's go." The phone went silent, this time for keeps.

Lisa closed her eyes and began to tug at a thick lock of her blonde hair. "Oh, God, please let him be OK."

# Chapter 2 - Break out the Scotch

Tim was tapping away at Hoyt's phone, looking for more information. He'd quickly found a dozen recordings under the voice memo app. One was labeled French, another Arabic and a third labeled Italian. Other recordings were marked as trading tips, the Constitution, advanced mathematics. One was labeled "Harry Potter."

All had older dates. However, the one that caught Tim's attention was dated just three days ago and said "DANGER." Of course, he pushed that one.

"If you are listening to this recording, you are in danger. You are in danger of knowing too much." Hoyt could be a bit of an alarmist. "I have discovered the secret to rapid and long-term learning. You are not yet ready to comprehend the implications of this technology and neither is the rest of the world. Your discretion is required. Imagine for a moment that you could memorize anything you hear, Spanish, German, Italian, the Constitution, a complex manual, all in the time that it takes you to hear it. My vision was for people to be able to order downloadable training manuals, learn languages, listen to virtually any course once and retain everything."

"Good: if we all spoke multiple languages, I would think we would communicate better.

"Bad: we would become a race of superhumans as people strive to input more and more information. In addition to the disparity between rich and poor, we would also have a growing disparity between the educated and uneducated.

"Good: Car companies, or any company for that matter, could have every employee memorize safety and procedural manuals, increasing safety and productivity. Students could hear a lesson once and retain everything.

"Bad: commercials on TV could use this technology and we wouldn't know. We would wonder why we were always singing their jingle and knew everything about their product.

Tim clicked the pause button and went into deep thought. He stared right past Lisa and started to mumble under his breath. "So, you could hear the sound of a bird, an insect—hell, anything—and then be told what that sound was and in the future be able to identify that sound with complete recollection."

Lisa joined in, "People could become experts in any field almost instantly. They could learn any language." She pondered a moment and let out an uncomfortable chuckle. "Italian."

Tim continued off in another odd direction. "You could be trained to hear a gunshot, followed by the definition of the gun type and its capabilities, and identify it. Imagine a police force with that capability. Imagine an army with that capability. They hear a 'crack' off in the distance and immediately know 'That's a semi-automatic AK-47 7.62 x 39 mm assault rifle with a range of—'"

Lisa interrupted Tim. "Play the tape, please. I would like to find my husband."

Hoyt's voice continued. "People could become experts in any field almost instantly. Famous speeches could be memorized word for word. Every man, woman and child would know the Constitution, the Bible, the Koran. Imagine the ramifications of extremists touting their understanding of any verse of any religion. Any book ever written could be stored in memory." Hoyt was quiet for a moment as if pondering. "I wonder if we're like computers and have limited space." Hoyt could be heard chuckling through his nose. "What if someone tried to input too much information? Would they go nuts? What if you downloaded information that you just wanted to forget? Could you? I don't know. This technology just isn't ready for the mainstream . . . And it's heading there, anyway. If this kind of technology gets out in the open, we would have to . . ." Hoyt may have finished this sentence in his head, but not on the tape, leaving Tim wondering what he was thinking. After ten long seconds of silence, Hoyt continued, "We would have to guard our ears from everything we hear. Someone would no doubt think to hide the inaudible high pitch within a message in an attempt to infiltrate our mind. There's also the danger of the high-pitched tone. In early tests, I suffered temporary hearing loss. I have since turned down the pitch to a safer level. So many things can go wrong. Ask yourself: what would you learn if you had the ability to hear it once and retain it forever? I was trying to figure out a way to learn while I slept, but maintaining a heart rate of 120 was an issue. I think I have since come up with a way to maintain a heart rate of 120 for short periods of time through medication. However, I'm concerned about maintaining a heart rate unnaturally for any length of time. One of the great outcomes of this study for me has been getting into great shape. The research has got me up to four hours a day on the treadmill. I find that I'm having to run longer and harder to maintain a natural heart rate of 120 bpm as I get into better and better condition. Maybe that's a good thing. Maybe the amount that we learn should be limited to our effort."

Hoyt's recording was momentarily silent. "I think I'll invest in treadmills."

Lisa took the moment to comment. "So, now he's an investor."

The tape continued. "To do the program right, doctor supervision would be necessary. This is not a one-size-fits-all. Making it available only to the privileged few who can afford the equipment required to monitor vitamin and mineral levels, blood levels, heart rate, et cetera, would be a travesty." Hoyt was rambling but by now he had Tim's full attention. "In a perfect world, someone would have to be in charge of the kind of information that would be able to be created and distributed with the high-pitched tone. But human nature has taught us that this will get out and be misused. Is it a gift . . . or a curse? Would we be forced to test it on monkeys first? Is this the technology that finally makes the Planet of the Apes a reality? I imagine a future where everyone holds a pitch-tone machine the size of an iPhone; or better yet, the tone is an app, and every time we expect to say or hear something we deem to be important, we could push the pitch button so we never forget what was said. Could someone's recollection of what someone said be used in court? Doctors could be trained in just one year. The role of a teacher would either change or become obsolete. How long before someone tries to re-create what I've done and screws up somebody for life? I can see lawsuits for people losing their hearing or dying on the treadmill while trying to maintain 120 bpm for hours on end. I imagine in the future people selling cloud accounts. Selling pitch-infused information, priced by the megabyte." Finally, the phone went silent. After waiting to be sure Hoyt was really finished, Tim took a moment to mentally summarize everything he'd heard. Lisa motioned for Tim to follow her to the kitchen. She reached into the back of a tall cabinet and fished out a bottle. Tim recognized the 25-year-old Scotch that Hoyt saved for very special occasions or severe depression. Lisa poured herself a tall drink.

Tim began his recap. "The magic is in the heart rate, nutrition, and some kind of high-pitch tone." But he quickly shifted to thinking about how Hoyt had been acting.

He mumbled, "He called me last week; sounded freaked out. A bit paranoid. He had something he wanted to tell me. Something he wanted to show me. He made me promise to come for the weekend or take some time off work. Not so easy."

Tim mentally ticked off the essential facts in Hoyt's life recently. That he owns a cutting-edge laboratory in the city. He's a well-respected businessman. A brilliant biochemist. But much to his disappointment, his laboratory had become more of a vitamin warehouse. Hoyt's business now specialized in custom blends of high-end vitamins. Hoyt's small staff works weekdays from 8 to 4 but most of the magical blending and technical tweaking happened after hours or on the weekend. In short: what Hoyt was up to these days took place out of sight from his staff. And Hoyt had complained that his employees had recently become more and more inquisitive.

Lisa perched on the edge of the couch, Scotch in

hand. The broken coffee table left her without a place to set her drink. She clutched the glass tightly, taking sip after sip, silently shaking her head in disbelief.

# Chapter 3 - Meet the Hired Guns

While Tim was silently watching Lisa nursing her drink, the two guys who'd roughed her up were keeping an eye on the house. They were parked in the street near the end of the driveway. The smaller of the two was named Louis. He's a street punk, a wanna-be thug. He'd been orphaned at the age of six when his single mother died of an overdose. He was bounced from orphanage to orphanage before finally being adopted briefly at age eight. That ended quickly. He'd been returned to the orphanage two weeks later after starting a fire in his bedroom. At age sixteen, he'd been assigned to a work program, from which he ran away at his first opportunity. Now he runs money or drugs for a career criminal named Carlos. Louis always has his gun out. His favorite line is, "I will fuckin' shoot you." Carlos has had a soft spot for Louis ever since Louis shot a guy who had a knife to Carlos' throat during a deal gone bad.

Paul was a bigger guy, five feet 11, maybe six feet even, and pushing 250 pounds. He looks like he used to pump weights back in the day. A big chest, but a soft layer of fat all the way around. Likes to eat and always has a can of Coke in his hand. A burger and a fry kind of guy. Ethnic, maybe a mix of Spanish and Italian. Looks like a bigger version of Tony Soprano.

Louis and Paul were originally supposed to take Lisa, not Hoyt, but Hoyt messed up that plan by being home. He'd sneaked in the back door about 11:30 that night so he could lie to Lisa about how late he'd gotten home. Having Hoyt instead of Lisa had seriously complicated things.

And so, Paul was sent back to get Lisa. But since Tim had driven her back from the police station and gone back into the house with her, plan C was put into effect. It started out with a phone call.

* * *

Lisa's cell phone jingle played its familiar tune, but she ignored it for two or three rings. Then, suddenly, she jumped to attention, looking first for a place to set her drink and then rummaging for her phone. "Hello. . . . hello." After a moment of silence, a strong deep voice spoke, loud enough to make her pull the phone a few inches from her ear.

"Hello, Lisa. I think you've been waiting for this call." Stunned, Lisa remained silent for a moment, waving her hand violently to get Tim's attention. She held the phone to her chest as if that would mute her voice and mouthed the words "It's them" to Tim.

"Are you listening? Because I'm only going to say this once."

Lisa clapped the phone back against her face. She thought the caller wouldn't know Tim was present. The voice went on. "We have Hoyt, and he is fine for the moment. We are the guys that lent him almost a million dollars to develop his . . . well . . . 'The Gift' as we are calling it." Lisa pulled the phone away from her ear and tapped the speaker button. She took two steps away from the phone as if distancing herself kept her safer. Tim motioned for her to stay close, hoping the caller couldn't tell the phone was on speaker. The voice continued. "Things have not moved along as fast as we were promised, and we are going to need to collect."

Lisa spoke up in a high-pitched, apologetic voice. "What does that mean? I don't have that kind of money." Tim was pressing one finger to his lips and silently mouthed the words, "Just listen." Pulling out his phone, Tim hit the record button and laid his phone next to Lisa's.

The stern voice continued, "Stop talking and listen."

She did as the voice told her.

"We are willing to forget the money that your husband owes us in exchange for the work he has done to this point. Once he has gathered all the notes and handed over all the equipment, we will have him legally sign over the rights to the patents. We will compensate you and your husband handsomely for your time and effort. However: if you involve the police or mess up this deal in any way, your husband will have an unfortunate accident. All you need to do is have patience. Can you do that?"

Tim nodded vigorously, indicating she should answer yes.

"Yes. . . . Please, don't hurt him," she squeaked, a trembling hand between her breasts trying to keep her pounding heart from beating out of her chest.

"That's up to you." The phone went silent for a moment and then the voice continued. "How about you, Tim? That okay with you?"

Tim's head snapped up from the two phones he'd been staring at. His eyes met Lisa's.

The voice wasn't finished. "Did you find the police a little less cooperative than you expected?"

Tim kept silent.

"Why don't you go home and feed your dog, maybe pick up a few groceries for Lisa. We're going to need her to stay put. We just need a few days to get all the legalities in order and this can be a win-win situation for everybody."

Tim finally spoke up. "If this is such a win-win for everybody, why is Hoyt being held against his will?"

Whoever this was, he knew how to keep his cool. The response was calm but firm. "Let's just say he needed an incentive to get the job done faster."

Tim spoke again. "Can you elaborate on this win-win analogy?"

This time, after three, maybe four seconds of silence, the man replied, speaking slowly but agitation evidence in his voice. "No. You were not part of this plan and frankly, you are already starting to annoy me. Go about your business, but know that we will have eyes on you. At this house, at your house. Hell, we'll know if you buy regular or skim milk at the store." At this, Tim realized, he was seeing real fear in Lisa's eyes.

"There is more at stake than you realize, more at stake than Hoyt realizes." The voice paused for a moment or two. "Your new job is to keep Lisa calm. Two days and everybody retires. Can I count on your cooperation, Tim?"

Tim's head and facial expressions said *yes*

moments before his cautious verbal response. "Yes."

The caller concluded with more instructions. "Lisa, keep your phone close by. Answer when I call. Understand?"

Her voice shaky, Lisa responded, "I understand."

"Nothing stupid, and you and your husband live happily ever after." The connection was lost.

Tim tapped the stop button on his cell phone, which had recorded most of the conversation. He was already anxious to replay the recording. Did he have a confession of guilt? Or anything, he hoped, that proved who was holding Hoyt captive? Anything at all that could hold up in court?

Lisa finally spoke. "So. What, we do nothing?"

Tim remained quiet, but the wheels were turning. His eyes focused on the floor for a good long time and then he stood up and went right for Lisa's and Hoyt's bedroom. "I think they originally came for you. They might still come for you. Why else would they let me leave but insist that you stay?" Tim scanned every corner of the bedroom and then returned to the living room. "Do you have a gun in the house?"

"No, we never needed a gun," Lisa said. Then, after a long pause, "You're scaring me."

"Good. You should be scared," Tim said. "These guys are serious. Are you sure Hoyt doesn't have any weapons? Knife? Bat? Nunchucks?"

Lisa stopped in her tracks and then locked eyes on her purse. "I have a Taser. Hoyt just got it for me about a month ago." She began to move items around in her big purse for a bit too long for Tim's liking. He grabbed it from her and dumped it onto the kitchen counter.

Among the assortment of seemingly useless items were mini sample-size hair and skin products, half a pack of chewing gum, a breath sprayer, hair brush, a compact, mini tissue pack, lipstick shade number one, lipstick shade number two, colorful ladies' wallet able to hold a dozen credit cards—and one mini Taser. Tim held it up as if he just solved a mystery.

Lisa responded sarcastically. "Yeah, nice job, Sherlock. I never would have found it."

Tim eyed up the tiny gadget, flipping it from one side to the other. "He sent me the same one in the mail; about three weeks ago."

"Give it here!" Lisa snapped, snagging it from his hand. She slid a small button up to the "on" position and pointed it in Tim's direction. It zapped unimpressively for half a second and continued to hum. But no lightning bolts. "Crap. It's dead. I was supposed to charge it." Tim was reaching for it but Lisa pulled it back, turning her body enough to give Tim the message: *Back off, I got this.* She flipped up the built-in charging plug and pushed the mini Taser into the outlet by the sink, right next to her fancy toaster and the designer knife block. Tim caught Lisa also staring at the assortment of knife handles. He could see her imagining a bloody stab fest, just like he was. Lisa spoke up first. "I'm not stabbing anyone, but I don't want to be stabbed, either." She grabbed the heavy wooden block and stashed the whole set under the sink. Opening the silverware drawer, she scooped up the remaining knives, moved them into the drawer below and covered them with oven mitts.

"What about a tool box? Please tell me Hoyt has a tool box."

Lisa's eyes made a bee-line for a nearby closet. "Well, his tools are at the lab. But I have a toolbox."

Tim snapped his head back in surprise. He'd never considered Lisa "The handy type." "Really? You have a toolbox?"

Lisa was quick with her middle finger and an evil stare. "There is more to me than just what Hoyt tells you." Lisa's hands went to her hips. "Who do you think fixes things around here? Hoyt's always at the lab or in his office. I would surprise you."

Tim inched back the curtains to see if he could make out anyone watching the house. He instantly spotted a black Cadillac SUV with dark windows and vapor puffing out of its muffler. Nearby sat a white minivan with some generic air conditioning company's logo. The house was next to a forest preserve on one side, making it fairly private. The house on the other side was up for sale and empty, which made this place almost secluded. The next house with inhabitants was two doors down. Lisa said she and Hoyt had never gotten past a friendly hello in the two years since those new neighbors moved in.

The garage was detached and its big overhead door, as well as the side door, were in view of the two vehicles on the street. Tim eased the curtains shut and looked back in Lisa's direction. "Let me see your toolbox."

* * *

Tim was right. Paul had been instructed to

monitor the house to see if either Tim or Lisa went anywhere.

Louis' orders were to go back to the abandoned storage facility to check on Hoyt.

\* \* \*

Hoyt had been left in the dark since about 2 a.m. He was trying to piece the details of his evening back together. Any recollection of the drive, to wherever he was, evaded him. He remembered being manhandled out of a vehicle and struggling to stay on his feet. Two men had dragged him along like the drunken friend who'd had one, maybe two, too many drinks. They must have drugged him, he realized. He remembered that the bigger guy had held him up against a cold, wet wall of some kind while the other seemed to be trying to unlock something.

Hoyt remembered the fresh air and movement bringing back a little clarity and that he'd attempted to wrestle his way free from a pair of big hands and a vise-like grip. A flashlight had been pointed in their direction, making the big guy react. "Get that fuckin' light outa my face and open the door." How did he know the big guy's name was Paul? Maybe he'd overheard some conversation at some point in his ordeal. Anyway, Hoyt remembered, Paul had him up against the wall and up on his tip toes. Paul's tight grip on the neck of Hoyt's hooded sweatshirt was making him gag. He had been preparing for a run on his office treadmill. And because Lisa liked to keep the house at a chilly sixty-nine degrees, he'd started out, as he always did, with the hoodie as a warm-up outfit. But while the big thug had him up against the wall, his hood had been pulled over his head, giving him only moments of vision out of just one eye. The other guy—was his name Louis? Yeah, Louis, he was pretty sure—had finally gotten the lock open and begun to tug on a chain that lifted a noisy overhead door. When the door was opened, just enough, Hoyt's head had been tucked down and he was shoved inside. The headlights of the vehicle he'd ridden in exposed the insides of some sort of storage building.

Hoyt's momentum was stopped by the horizontal railings of an old open-bed trailer, which briefly knocked the wind out of him. The clanking of the chain alerted him to turn around in time to watch the headlights of the vehicle disappear as the door closed. "Hey! Hey! Let me out of here."

The last words his captor spoke to him were, "Scream away, old man. No one will hear you out here."

*Out here? Out where?* Hoyt closed his eyes and listened. He listened for every sound he could hear. If his experiments had taught him anything, it was that an accelerated heart rate could be used to your advantage. The bigger guy had told the smaller guy to shut up and lock the door. *Note: there are two guys. Note: Both voices are now locked into memory.* He heard the two men near the left side of the roll-down door. Their shoes seemed to be kicking small stones. A beam of light peeked under the corner of the door from the flashlight that had been used to locate the lock.

"Check it," said the big voice.

"It's locked," responded the smaller voice.

Hoyt could hear one of them rattle the lock and then attempt to open the door. "Let's go. Carlos has called twice already." Hoyt expected that Carlos was behind the abduction, but couldn't be sure he was the actual ringleader. Two sets of footsteps faded away toward the vehicle. He could tell the bigger guy went to the driver's side and the smaller guy went left. *Note: Bigger guy driving.* The left door had a slight squeak, as if not used very often. He could tell that the windows were rolled up by the muffled and solid sound of craftsmanship made when the doors closed. When the car started, he was sure it was an SUV: a high-end SUV, like an Escalade or Infinity. He heard the wheels spin, spitting gravel, as the vehicle backed up and turned, taking with it the last bit of light. After a moment of silence, more gravel spitting as the car moved forward. The crunch of tires on gravel got quieter and quieter. One last distant burst of power, and the engine accelerating through the gears, suggested that a long driveway off a freeway or at least a road able to tolerate fifty, maybe sixty miles per hour. And then: what others might call silence. But Hoyt's trained ear detected a mix of crickets and frogs. The smaller frogs and crickets dominated the choir while bigger frogs added occasional bass. A slight buzzing of electricity—*Note: Power line nearby*—filled the few moments when the night creatures took a break. An occasional car was just barely audible but obviously passing at a pretty fast pace and way off in the distance. Hoyt briefly tried beating on the door and yelling but he already knew he was going to have to think his way out.

He sat on the edge of the trailer trying to figure out why he had been taken. Surely someone would come back to let him know. He knew it was likely related to The Gift. He had been warned that he was running out of time to pay back his hard-money lenders. He'd had no choice but to borrow the money.

He was so close to discovering the secret to limitless learning, and yet banks weren't interested in his theories. They wanted too much information even to consider the loan. His latest ideas were ground-breaking, but the patents hadn't been secured yet. The packaging of old and new ideas and the addition of his latest discovery was a game changer but certainly not rocket science. The patent was everything.

Originally Hoyt had thought his success was related to heart rate, but upon further testing he discovered it was more about the volume of blood flow. The high heart rate created the needed blood flow. Hoyt had spent the last few weeks with a brilliant neurosurgeon, Dr. Robert Bimlik. This expert confirmed that a perfectly functioning brain was capable of amazing feats. We have all seen the videos of someone using their mind to bend a spoon and to make a pen stand up on its tip and spin. Bimlik had assured Hoyt that complete recollection was not only plausible but the purpose of a perfectly functioning human brain. He'd explained how the cerebrum is divided into two equal hemispheres that control our thoughts and actions. He spoke in fairly elementary terms but as long as Hoyt didn't interrupt him, he would verify many of his findings. "It's the largest part of the brain and consists of four lobes. The parietal is responsible for recognition, movement, orientation and perception of stimuli." Hoyt nodded his head respectfully and professor Bimlik continued. "The frontal lobe assists us with problem solving, planning, reasoning and such. The occipital lobe controls our sense of sight. Last, but not least and certainly of the most interest to you," he continued, "the temporal lobe controls memory, speech and perception of auditory stimuli." Finally, he was getting to what Hoyt wanted to hear—needed to hear. "Equally important is the hippocampus, which is responsible for long-term memory." Where the doctor got into completely unfamiliar territory for Hoyt was about the three main arteries feeding the brain. "When these arteries are functioning at 100 percent, they are capable of stimulating the suritolic stem." He dumbed it down for Hoyt by referring to this as the "cerebral clitoris." He explained his joke by commenting, "Very hard to find but difficult to stop playing with once found." Hoyt's drive for perfect health through nutrition and his outstanding blood flow made him a perfect candidate to test this hypothesis. Once the door to his "cerebral clitoris" was open, he stimulated it further with a 110 kiloherz tone, not only waking this rarely stimulated organ, but teasing it with childlike curiosity for more, more, more.

With Hoyt's notes, others could develop the product. Hoyt certainly wasn't ready to start blabbing his findings all over town, especially with patents still pending. During his frustrating search for funding, one of the bank representatives had confided in him about a hard-money lender who was pretty lenient. But when Hoyt met that shadowy figure, he told Hoyt that science wasn't his area of expertise; he was "more of a real estate investor." However, he knew a guy who might be interested. And that's how Hoyt came to know Carlos. He was the guy who knew a hard-money lender who knew a banker. What could go wrong?

It had been about four months ago that Hoyt first spoke to Carlos on the phone. They'd set up an appointment to meet at the lab on a Sunday afternoon. Carlos showed up with his partner Frank, who was accompanied by his wife Brenda. Hoyt put on a nice dog-and-pony show, explaining how he was able to learn three languages in three weeks or quote verbatim from a complex manual. He asked Brenda to open to any page out of the two-inch thick Harry Potter book that sat on the metal laboratory table, explaining that he could quote every word. Brenda feathered through the book and stopped about a quarter of the way through. "Page 256," she said, in an accent that suggested a northeastern origin, perhaps Brooklyn. Hoyt began to recite.

A couple of paragraphs in, Carlos stopped him. "Look, you can't con a con artist. These are simple parlor tricks. Stop wasting my time and show me some proof."

Hoyt assured them all that he had not possessed any of this knowledge three weeks earlier. "If I hear it, I can recall it from memory. So could you."

"Prove it to me. Show me how you do it."

Hoyt held up a finger, telling them to stay put. He went to the back of the lab and pulled a lanyard from a hook on the wall. The lanyard held an electronic door card. His visitors watched him disappear into a room marked "DANGER Biohazard, Authorized Personnel Only." When he reappeared, he held a small device, the size of a cell phone. He plugged it into a box the size of a microwave on the lab table. He pushed a button, which lit up a few diodes, and began to twist and adjust two knobs on the machine. Next he plugged a nice, sound-muffling headset into the device and held it out to Carlos. He accepted the phones, which looked like oversized earmuffs, and nudged his head upward towards Hoyt, indicating he expected further explanation. "I am currently modifying a simple hearing aid that will be designed to emit the high pitch that opens the cerebral clit . . ." Hoyt hesitated. "Cerebral sensors. Go ahead, put them on." Hoyt hoped his tone was reassuring. Carlos eased them over his bald head, never taking his gaze off Hoyt. Hoyt shook off the ominous feeling he got from Carlos' cold eyes and pushed a button, releasing a high-pitched tone. Carlos listened for a moment and took off the headset, looking very unimpressed. Hoyt could see he had plenty of explaining to do. The actual pitch he uses is nearly inaudible, of course, but he figured a headset that made no noise would be even less impressive. "The blood flow opens the door to the mind," he told Carlos. "The high pitch stimulates the organ that helps you remember." Hoyt began to recap, trying to keep it easy enough for his audience to understand but detailed enough for them to know this wasn't a magic pill.

Thirty more minutes into the sales pitch, Carlos cut him off. He asked Hoyt how much money he needed to finish the project. When Hoyt told him $800,000, Carlos didn't blink. "How long before it's ready for market?" Hoyt rattled off a list of red-tape reasons why it was still two years away from a very select and limited rollout. Carlos laughed and restated his question. "How long before it's black-market ready?"

Despite having such detailed recollections to occupy his mind, the hours passed slowly in the hot shed. Hoyt quickly grew tired of stumbling around in the pitch black. He was able to figure out that the back and side walls were cement and the only way out was through the industrial-strength roll-up door. It was locked from the outside. Some kind of an open trailer took up most of the space. When the door had been opened to shove him in, he remembered seeing that the big trailer had boards missing. It was as if someone was in the middle of tearing off the old rotting timber to replace it with new wood. He discovered boards randomly scattered on the cracked cement floor, making it hard to shuffle around in the dark without tripping. Along one side ran a metal shelf about six feet tall. From the smell of gas and oil, he assumed there was a chain saw, a weed whacker or at least a gas can stored somewhere on the shelves. Leaning against the shelves was a shovel. He suddenly wished he had listened to and memorized every episode of *MacGyver*. He slammed his fist, hard, on the corrugated metal door. He heard a noise he hadn't noticed before. Another rap on the door was followed, again, by a "tink." Again: "rap" . . . and a corresponding "tink." Hoyt continued to rap on the door and systematically made his way to the noise. He followed the sound to the door's right edge. There he found a key drop. The hinged flap was about two inches tall and six inches wide. Designed for keys and folded paperwork, he assumed. A look out of the key drop showed a few dim lights screened behind thick brush. Using a sliver of wood from the floor, he propped the hinged flap open, hoping to let new air in and to hear better.

First thing he heard was an occasional car, whipping by at a pretty fast clip. Too far away to hear any of Hoyt's yelling. The beat-up old trailer took up most of the room, preventing him from getting up the head of steam it would require to even attempt to derail the twelve-foot-wide industrial door.

After endlessly pondering alternatives, he noticed a ray of light coming through the propped-open key drop. *Finally. Morning.* Soon afterward, Hoyt heard a vehicle approach the warehouse. Peeking out of the key drop, he began to yell as the truck got closer but silenced himself as it pulled right up the front and stopped. He couldn't see above the waist of the person who got out. Dirty work boots and worn-out blue jeans walked past the key drop and stopped at the door's opposite end. The man jiggled the lock and inserted a key. Hoyt grabbed the shovel he'd found earlier and prepared for battle.

Before twisting the key to unlock the door, the man spoke. "I am about to remove this lock. I am going to ask you to pull the chain and slowly lift this door. While you are lifting the door, I will be stepping back to get a good aim at you. Make no mistake: I will shoot you and not lose a bit of sleep. Understand?"

To which Hoyt replied, "Understand." He recognized the voice as that of the smaller man from last night. Louis was his name. Hoyt put down the shovel and felt around for the chain; he'd already discovered and tested it. This time it moved. Pulling hand over hand, he steadily raised the overhead door, revealing a tall, thin outline of a man with a big pistol pointing right at him.

The sun was surprisingly bright. Hoyt shielded his eyes while they adjusted to the light. He made yet another mental note. *Based on the sunrise, the building is facing east.* He tried to make out details of his captor but the bright sun behind him made him look like little more than a shadow. His analytical moment was interrupted by Louis's twangy voice. "Go to the back of the shed." With his pistol, Louis pointed to of the space behind the trailer. Hoyt hesitated for just a moment and Louis took the opportunity to use his signature phrase. He looked all animated and crazy. "I will fuckin' shoot you." Hoyt complied, with one hand over his head and the other shielding the direct sunlight. "Get down on your knees." Louis backed up slowly, keeping one eye on Hoyt and the other on the back of his truck, an older Chevy. He reached into the bed and struggled to pull a green five-gallon bucket over the side. He walked the bucket around the trailer with a disturbing grin on his face. He kept the gun aimed at Hoyt as he put the bucket down at Hoyt's feet. He tapped the gun right up against Hoyt's head and softly said, "Boom."

Hoyt's first thought was, *Bang, you idiot, not boom.* His eyes closed tightly and stayed shut until Louis eased the gun away from his head. Louis took five steps back and spit a brown mess of chewing tobacco on the filthy concrete near the bucket. "This is for you."

Hoyt looked at the bucket and then back at Louis. "What is it?"

Louis' smile had a sinister look. "It's your leash." Then he wiggled the pistol back and forth between the bucket and Hoyt indicating for Hoyt to go ahead: look inside. Inside was a twelve-foot length of chain and two padlocks. Louis instructed him to wrap the chain around the trailer's frame and click the lock shut. "Now wrap the other end around your ankle." Hoyt wrapped the chain around his ankle and proceeded to slip the lock through two of the links. "Tighter." Louis insisted on using his pistol like an index finger. Once Hoyt was secure, Louis made his way back to the front of the shed. There, he put one foot up on the trailer and leaned on his knee. "You best get comfortable; you might be here for a while." Louis finally tucked his pistol into the back of his pants, hidden by his dirty flannel shirt.

Hoyt stood up. "Wait, are you leaving?"

"Yup."

"Wait, please. Why am I here? I need food; I have to use the bathroom."

Louis gave his unpleasant smile again, and glanced toward the green bucket. "You didn't think that bucket was just for carrying stuff in, did you? That's a top-o'-the-line model toilet. When you're not using it to do your business, you can flip it over and use it for a chair." He laughed. Hoyt slumped at the reality of his situation.

"Quit your crying. I'll be back." Louis cranked the door three-quarters of the way down from the inside, and ducked under it.

Hoyt watched the man disappear, from the waist down, darkening the hell hole once again. He listened to Louis place the lock on the far end of the door. As if being chained up wasn't enough.

# Chapter 4 -  Shed Some Light

At the police station, things were finally calming down. Sergeant Jenkins was just wrapping up a conversation with one of his precinct's paper pushers. As he left the office, Jenkins blurted out, "Oh, yeah, send a black and white to the Pendleton house." The man pushed up his glasses and held the door open. His "deer in the headlights" expression prompted a response from the sergeant. "The lady that said someone took her husband." The man's blank stare continued. "Brunette. Bandages on her face." He hesitated as Officer Cleveland walked by. When he thought she was out of earshot, he continued. "Frilly red top; tight jeans." Noticing that he had caught Officer Cleveland's attention, he lowered his voice. Covering the side of his mouth, he whispered, "Big boobs."

"Oh, yeah!" the guy brightened right up. "Her!"

Officer Cleveland chimed in. "I heard that." She turned to face officer Melbern, who was preoccupied with the last oversized bite of his jelly donut, followed by noisy finger licking. "Andy." No response. "Andy Melbern."

Finally, Melbern's head popped up. He snatched up his Dunkin Donuts napkin and wiped his mouth. He managed to mumble, "What?" still chewing and wiping his mouth, leaning over his desk so the crumbs wouldn't fall to the floor.

Officer Cleveland just stared at him in disgust. "You're worse than the stereotype."

He repeated his brilliant response. "What?"

She continued, "Boss wants a black and white to the Pendleton house."

He tilted his head like a confused dog, prompting a deep sigh from Officer Cleveland. She looked at Sergeant Jenkins, who was still trying to listen in from his office, and she repeated his earlier description. "You know, brunette, frilly red top, tight jeans, big boobs." Jenkins shrugged his shoulders apologetically and waved to his staff guy to let his office door close.

Officer Prissue jumped up. "I'll go. I'm gonna go crazy if I have to spend another minute behind this desk."

Officer Cleveland quickly shut him down. He was the new cop. A rich kid who dressed the part and spoke the vernacular but just wasn't cop material. They often referred to him as Richie Rich. "Nope, not this time, rookie. Andy and I already interrogated this lady. Pretty sure it's just a domestic thing. We'll check out her place, do a little drive around the neighborhood and bring back some pizza."

The newbie sat down, his face telegraphing his disappointment that he wouldn't be leaving the precinct. He did nod his head in approval regarding the pizza. "Pepperoni, please."

\* \* \*

Tim and Lisa had made pretty good progress securing the house. All doors and windows were locked, and barbaric weapons strategically deployed around the house. Tim insisted that Lisa get an undersized wire snipper from her craft kit and tape it to her calf. "Hoyt is probably cuffed with zip ties right now, wishing he had . . ." Tim stopped himself when he saw the look in Lisa's eyes. He finished with, "Let's just be ready for anything."

She was way ahead of his next instruction: "We need to find you a hiding place." Lisa already had her hideaway picked out. The house had a formal dining room but also a breakfast nook just off the kitchen, with corner windows overlooking the side of the house. The nook held two custom wicker benches with mitered corners that met to form the corner. Lisa had seen them online and liked that they had storage space inside for extra blankets and pillows. Last year, when her 8-year-old niece came for a weekend visit, they had played hide and seek. Her niece hid in the wicker bench and fell fast asleep. After an hour of searching Lisa called the police. By the time they arrived she was inconsolable, just repeating herself: "My brother is going to kill me. He's gonna kill me. She was right here! We were playing hide and seek and now she's gone!" When little Andrea popped her sleepy head up from inside the wicker bench, Lisa saw the two cops look at each other with that stupid look cops give each other just before they say something profound like "Uh huh." It didn't help that the same two cops showed up at the house only a month ago when one of her arguments with Hoyt made its way out into the driveway. An uppity neighbor walking her dog thought calling the cops was the neighborly thing to do.

Lisa pulled the table out another foot, so she could lift off the cushioned seat cover and prepare her new quarters. Tim convinced her she needed to sleep there in case somebody tried to snag her in the middle of the night. She quickly became obsessed with her new wicker bed. She lined the bottom with a soft comforter and her favorite pillow. She stuffed snack bars under the pillow and arranged weapons and a flashlight along the sides. Her weapons of choice were her fully charged tiny Taser and an oversized pair of fabric scissors, another borrowing from her craft kit. She liked that she could fit three fingers into the handle. It made her feel less likely to lose it in the unlikely event she would actually use it. She imagined herself lying on her back with the Taser in one hand and the scissors in the other. She simulated a couple of awkward stabs that gave Tim very little confidence she could fend off an attacker. He put his hand out and flicked his fingers in the universal signal for "Hand 'em over." With a couple of twists and a good pull Tim unhinged the scissors and handed her the top half. The half with the bigger handle. "Now you can stab or swipe."

Tim instructed her to keep her cell phone with her at all times, but it had to be on silent and the vibration off. "But what if they try to call me or Hoyt calls me?"

Tim's response left her deeply unsettled. "What if they break in and can't find you? It's just like when you can't find your own phone. They'll call you and hear your phone ring or vibrate. And then, instead of hiding, you're just trapped."

She made the adjustments to her phone and then made it magically disappear inside her bra.

A knock on the door startled her. Tim already had her paranoid enough, but she noticed that he jumped, too. Oddly enough, the threatening earlier call had actually been settling to her. The stern voice through the phone was reassuring. She could still hear the man saying, "All you need to do is have patience. Can you do that?"

The second knock on the door was louder, followed by a male voice. "Police, Mrs. Pendleton, following up from this morning." A hundred thoughts went through Lisa's head. *Are these cops involved? If they think it's a domestic issue, are they going to assume that Tim is the "other guy?" Is it really even the cops out there? Are the thugs watching, thinking that we called the cops?*

Finally, a calming voice, which Lisa recognized as Officer Cleveland. "Lisa, we told you we would keep an eye on the place. Have you heard from your husband yet?"

Lisa looked at Tim hoping for some kind of input. He was frozen but looking around frantically. *He's thinking about hiding! But why? He hasn't done anything wrong.* Lisa finally spoke up. "Just a minute, let me put some clothes on." Tim instantly grimaced at this, giving her a reproachful look. Maybe that hadn't been the best sentence to buy time, she realized. She put the seat cover back over the wicker bench, pushed the wooden table back into place and straightened her frilly red top. Out of habit, she stopped in front of the small hallway mirror to check her hair and makeup. "How do I know it's really the police?" She thought the question was fair, seeing as someone broke into her house just the night before.

"I'm holding my badge to the eyehole, Mrs. Pendleton."

She put her eye to the peephole and recognized Officer Cleveland. Then she noticed the annoying

Officer Melbern. He looked even more disgusting through the peephole's distorting fish-eye lens. Her head drooped, and she looked back at Tim. He nodded. The door was about to open, and they hadn't yet planned for this moment. Tim took in a deep breath through his nose and held it. "Here goes nothing," he whispered, slowly releasing the breath through his mouth.

* * *

Louis had been instructed to "secure" Hoyt and then pick up Carlos for a personal visit to the storage shed. When they arrived, they discovered Hoyt was in bad shape. The space had reached a hundred ten degrees and was still pitch black. He had suffered a massive bout of diarrhea, likely from the anxiety, and appeared dehydrated. When Carlos and Louis opened the door, there was no sign of Hoyt. He was lying down behind the trailer. The stench from the bucket gagged Carlos. "Oh, my God. I told you to lock him up, not kill him. What did you do to him?"

"I didn't do anything to him, Carlos."

"Lock him up outside and clean this mess up. I can't get secrets from a dead man." Hoyt, who was barely conscious, seemed to perk up a bit when he heard Carlos' voice.

Louis fumbled through the keys on his keychain with one hand while burying his nose in the bend of his elbow. Carlos waved his hand back and forth past his nose. "Damn, boy, you stink." He headed back outside, leaving the dirty work to his grunt.

Louis slipped the key into the Master lock attached to the trailer and removed the lock from the chain. He held the chain like a leash and gave it two soft tugs. "Let's go, stinky." Hoyt was shielding his eyes from the light, taking very shallow breadths. Louis pulled on the chain again. "Get up." Holding the chain up, Louis directed Hoyt out into the sunlight. Carlos was already in the car, windows up and engine running to power the air conditioning, talking on the phone. He pushed the button to lower the passenger side window and yelled to Louis: "Bring him here." Louis walked Hoyt to the window like a dog. "I thought you wanted me to lock him up outside."

Carlos looked around. There was nowhere for Hoyt to run. Not in his current condition. "Get him in the car and go clean up that mess." Louis gathered up the long chain and handed it to Hoyt. He opened the door and motioned for him to get in. Hoyt eyed up the SUV before getting in, impressed that he'd been able to identify it as an Escalade yesterday just by hearing it start. Carlos switched his cell phone to his left hand and grabbed his sunglasses from the passenger seat. "Gotta go," he said to the person on the other end of the line. "Call you later with an update." The cold air felt good on Hoyt's now shirtless body but stung his overheated skin at the same time. He began to shiver uncontrollably. "Here, drink some water." Hoyt clutched at the bottle and downed half of it before beginning to choke and cough. "Slow down. I'm going to make sure you get some food and plenty of water. Sorry about Louis." Both Hoyt and Carlos took a moment to watch Louis come out of the storage shed with the green bucket full of piss and diarrhea, holding one hand over his mouth and nose. He made it three steps around the corner and chucked the bucket toward the back of the shed. "Good help is hard to find," Carlos said.

Hoyt dropped the armful of chain to the floor and finally spoke. "Where is Lisa?"

Carlos said nothing.

"I need food and I need to know why I'm here. I told you I was going to pay you back."

Carlos didn't respond and instead powered down his window, pinching his nose to shield himself from Hoyt's rank body odor. He yelled for Louis. "Hey, c'mere. Tie up your dog to the front of the trailer and go get us some burgers and fries."

Louis opened the passenger door and gathered up the chain again. "Let's go, puppy."

Carlos got out of the car, leaving it running. "Hurry up. It's hot as hell out here." Louis wrapped the long chain around the trailer's front hitch and clicked the lock, once again securing Hoyt. Now, at least, he was outside in the ninety-degree weather and somewhat fresh air.

A cloud shielded them from the burning sun for a moment and Carlos waved off Louis, reminding him, "Hurry up."

"Hoyt, Hoyt, Hoyt. I wish it didn't have to come to this. You know we have Lisa, too." He waited to see Hoyt's expression.

Hoyt was sitting on the trailer's tongue with his elbows resting on his knees to keep him from falling over. His body was quickly beading up with sweat. "There's no need to involve her. I'll give you what you want." He massaged his wet forehead and wiped away the stringy white foam that was forming at the corners of his lips.

"Good, then this should be nice and easy. You're going to sign over all the rights to 'The Gift' and give us all your notes, tips, tricks and toys. We're going to need to put on another little presentation, but this time we're going to put on a ten-million-dollar presentation. If you get me the sale, I will compensate you very well. If you fuck this up for me, your wife will have an unfortunate accident and we'll set your lab on fire. Are we clear?"

Hoyt was slow to respond, but finally croaked out, "We're clear."

Carlos handed him the bottle with his last few gulps of water. "Good. What do you need from me to make this happen two days from now?"

Hoyt lifted his head and stared at Carlos for a few seconds. The cloud that had blocked the sun passed and the sun beat back down on them both. "Let's start with some food and some decent accommodations."

# Chapter 5 - The Shit List

When Lisa opened the front door, Officer Cleveland greeted her with a forced smile. Officer Melbern stood behind her, swiping a finger full of sweat from his forehead and flicking it to the ground. He wiped the remaining residue on his pants while advancing into the house. "Mind if we come inside to talk?" He turned his fat body sideways to push past Lisa, as if that required less space than walking straight in. Officer Cleveland looked apologetic, as if to say, "Sorry, he's the partner I'm stuck with."

Once inside, Melbern spotted Tim and looked him up and down. "Oh, you found your missing husband?"

*Ten seconds*, Tim told himself, *and he already has Lisa angry.*

"No, this isn't my husband."

The officer smirked and continued. "Boyfriend?"

Officer Cleveland, looking around the house, calmly said, "Give it a rest" to her annoying fellow cop.

Tim offered up an explanation. "She doesn't want to be alone right now."

Officer Melbern was obviously looking at Lisa's impressive breasts before turning back to Tim. "You two sleeping together?"

Tim and Lisa chimed in almost in sync. "No!" Melbern looked like a mess, but certainly kept their attention while Officer Cleveland began to wander around the house. "I thought I heard you say you had to put some clothes on," he said. There it was, the one sentence Tim knew was going to come back and bite them both in the ass.

"We're not sleeping together. I'm her husband's best friend."

To which Melbern responded, "Uh huh." Every word that came out of his mouth was offensive.

Lisa, apparently recognizing that he was trying to distract her, turned to address Officer Cleveland. "Excuse me, can I help you?" Officer Cleveland was separating the remaining items from Lisa's purse that had been dumped onto the kitchen counter. Lisa offered up an explanation. "I was looking for my Taser."

The officer picked up one of the lipsticks, removed the top and twisted until the pink lipstick popped out like an excited puppy. "What do you think, Melbern? This my color?"

Lisa was furious now. "Why are you here?"

Officer Cleveland placed the lipstick down on the table and shot a very serious look at Lisa and then Tim. "Ms. Pendleton, I thought we were coming here to see if you'd found your husband, but I'm starting to think there's more going on than you're letting on to." Both Lisa and Tim were silent. "You thinking the same thing, Melbern?"

He was glad to put in his two cents' worth. "Nine times out of ten, it's the spouse."

Lisa's eyes were on fire. "Get out of my house!" Tim stood in front of the refrigerator, unable to speak. "Now!" she shouted.

Tim knew the cops had reason to be suspicious, and Lisa knew it too. He could tell she also knew they had no right to be in the house. *Maybe they're with the thugs and wanted to see if we'll crack.* Either way, Lisa had made it clear she wanted them out of the house now.

"Lots of holes in your story, ma'am," Officer Cleveland said as she headed out the door. "Better get your story straight."

The door closed, and Lisa slid the deadbolt home. "What did she mean by that?"

Tim was still frozen in front of the refrigerator. "Which part?"

Lisa headed straight for the Scotch. "Oh, now you can speak." She poured herself half a glass and pushed Tim aside to get ice cubes from the freezer door. "'Better get your story straight,'" she repeated bitterly, followed by two good long gulps of the fine whisky. She twitched her head in reaction to the Scotch going down and continued, "We can't trust them. They know! They're a part of this!"

Tim shook his head, overwhelmed by all this. "We need to stay calm," he finally squeezed out. "Maybe we just need to let them do their thing. Maybe they're telling the truth about taking care of us after Hoyt gives them the, the, 'The Gift.'"

Lisa drained her drink with a final big gulp and banged the empty glass on the counter, sending the ice cubes bouncing like dice. "We need a plan."

\* \* \*

Hoyt heard tires crunching over gravel. He began to salivate, anticipating a burger and fries, as the black Escalade came into sight. Carlos, who had waited with him, was back on the phone, just out of earshot, trying to get better cell service. When Carlos saw Louis approaching, he headed back towards the building. Hoyt tried to make out the conversation but, by the time he was able to hear, the words were meaningless. "Hello; hello. Hey, the cell reception is shit out here. Let me call you back in a few."

Louis stepped out of the car with a mouthful of fries, holding two bags of food from McDonalds. Hoyt inhaled deeply, taking in the aroma of salty fries and a meat-like substance on a soft bun. He could even smell the ketchup and the mustard. He couldn't wait to bite into the burger and crunch the pickle. Carlos tucked his phone into his back pocket and motioned for Louis to bring the bags to him. He opened one and wafted it under Hoyt's nose. "You and me have an understanding. Right?" Hoyt tried not to act over-excited but something about the desperation of his circumstance made him feel like he hadn't had food in days. In reality, Hoyt had eaten a decent breakfast yesterday but then worked right through lunch and dinner. He nervously tapped on his forehead, waiting for Carlos to give him permission to reach into the bag. He knew Carlos' type. Have to feel like they're in charge. Carlos shook the bag and nodded his head. "Go ahead. Eat."

Hoyt scarfed down a double cheeseburger with large fries and greedily sucked down a medium Coke. Moments later, he was around the corner puking. At least as far around the corner as his chain would let him go.

Louis was quick to comment. "I'm not cleaning that up."

Carlos chuckled. "You okay, Hoyt?"

He was silent. He had his eye on a scrap of rebar that was leaning against the outside wall. "Give me a minute. I ate too fast." He heard the two men start a conversation and took the opportunity to stick the foot-long steel rod into his sock.

Carlos handed him the other McDonald's bag. "Here, eat slowly. You're going to need to keep something down."

\* \* \*

Tim was preparing for a trip to his house to let his ten-year-old Boston terrier out and then bring him back to Lisa's. Max wasn't a big dog, but he was a snarling, growling monster to anyone trying to get into the house without Tim's approval. Tim had left home abruptly within minutes after getting the 5 a.m. call from Sergeant Jenkins. It was almost certain, since he'd missed his usual morning walk, that Max had already messed in the house. Tim spent most of the drive back to his house looking in the rear-view mirror. That guy on the phone, with his smooth but sinister voice, had gotten into his head. From the moment Tim unlatched Lisa's front door, he felt as if eyes were on him. The black Escalade was gone and so was the AC repair van. In its place now was a light blue Handyman repair van. Two blocks down, a white minivan was parked in the street with the engine running. *Probably just a soccer mom picking up a neighborhood kid.*

\* \* \*

Moments after Tim turned left, two men came out of the Handyman van, each with a tool belt and a screw gun. They walked to the back door and began driving in long screws to secure the door shut. They split up, screwing every window shut. Lisa followed them from window to window. "Why are you doing that?" She was worried that they were going to lock her in and start a fire. But the men didn't acknowledge her in any way as they methodically went about their business. She wanted to call 911 but that would put Hoyt in jeopardy. When they got to the front door and started driving screws there, it was clear they didn't want her to leave or for Tim to come back into the house. As fast as they'd showed up, they disappeared. Lisa paced back and forth like a caged animal, the half scissors in her left hand and her Taser in her right. She put the blade and the Taser on the table, stuck her hand deep into her bra and pulled out her phone. She tapped the first three numbers of Tim's cell and went blank. From the junk drawer in the kitchen she pulled out an old-school spiral notebook with phone numbers penciled in. They hadn't added a number to the book in years, but Tim had been a friend of Hoyt's since high school.

He picked up right away. "Hey, everything okay?"

"No! They locked me in here, and you out!"

Tim responded by stating the obvious. "Wait, we locked ourselves in. What do you mean they locked you in? Lisa? . . . Hello?"

Lisa was preoccupied, pulling back the blinds to see if the van was still parked out front, but finally answered. "They screwed the doors and windows shut."

"They what?" Tim responded as he made the final turn towards his house.

Lisa repeated herself. "They screwed every door and window shut!"

* * *

Tim pulled onto his street and spotted the black SUV already parked in front of his house. "Let me call you right back; they're at my house." Tim stopped about four houses down and watched. He was able to see one guy in the driver's seat; he had momentary thoughts of ramming the vehicle. Moments later he saw a second man coming down his driveway, obviously tucking a gun back into his trousers. "What the fuck," he whispered under his breath. The second man got into the passenger seat. They pulled the SUV up another two houses and settled in. Tim watched from a distance for another minute and decided he wasn't going to let these two lock him in the house or kill him. That guy on the phone had said Tim wasn't part of their plan. *Maybe they plan to kill me.* He backed into the closest driveway and turned around hoping they hadn't noticed him behind them. He drove for five minutes, making every turn he could, all the while watching his rear-view mirror. When he was convinced that he wasn't being followed, he pulled over and called Lisa back.

"Hello. . . . Yeah, there at my house. If they did anything to Max, I swear I'll kill them."

Lisa was silent. Tim realized his comment was insensitive, seeing as they had her husband. Tim changed the subject. "We can't call the cops; we can't call Hoyt." Both went silent for a long time before Tim had a thought. "Hey, the guy that called you! We can call him back and ask him what's going on. Ya know, tell him we're getting nervous."

He heard a long sigh through the phone. "Let me see how that's gonna go," Lisa said. "'Hi, Mr. Thug, we were wondering if you would give us an update.'"

A familiar ring tone filled the car. Tim looked around, on the passenger seat and then over his shoulder into the back seat. The noise was coming from his pocket. It was Hoyt's phone. He must have picked it up from Hoyt and Lisa's house. By the time he pulled it out, it had stopped ringing. Moments later the tone pinged, indicating that a message had been left. Tim's heart was pounding. Was it a friend, a colleague, or one of the thugs? He stared at the number, which began with 248. That area code didn't mean anything to him. He nervously tapped his nails on the dashboard, then remembered he still had Lisa on his own cell.

"Oh, sorry, that was Hoyt's phone."

Now Lisa sounded excited. "Hoyt called you?"

"No, I have his phone. Someone was calling him. Hey, what was the number that the guy called from today? Was it a 248 number?"

He heard nothing for a moment as Lisa was apparently checking her call logs. "Yes, 248-665-2365. Why would he call Hoyt?"

Tim thought about this for a moment. "Maybe he's just looking for Hoyt's phone."

"Did he leave a message?"

"Yes."

"Well, are you going to listen to it?"

Tim took a deep breath. "Yeah, hold on." Tap, tap, tap, concluding with the speaker button.

"Tim, we missed you at the house. Hoyt is requesting that we bring him his phone. As you know by now, there is information on there that could speed things up, you know, wrap this whole thing up faster. Why don't you bring it back to Lisa's house?" *Click.*

They were both silent, Tim playing out his own version of these people's end game, assuming Lisa was doing the same. "He doesn't know that I have Hoyt's phone. Not for sure." There was silence; uncomfortable silence. "What if it's true? What if Hoyt needs his phone to finish?" Again, silence. Tim consciously tried to be sensitive, to think about what he would say before just blurting it out. "What if they just want to kill me?" he asked Lisa. "Remember, I wasn't part of the plan. If Hoyt really needed his phone, why didn't he have Hoyt talk to me?"

\* \* \*

Carlos hung up his phone and walked back up the driveway towards Hoyt. "Your friend Tim gave us the slip."

This got Hoyt's attention. His head popped up. "Tim? Why are you involving Tim? He doesn't know anything."

Carlos sat uncomfortably close to Hoyt and spoke in a soft voice. "He does now."

Both men were silent, as happens while running scenarios through their heads. Carlos spoke first. "Here's what's going to happen, Hoyt. We are going to convert this little slice of heaven into your new lab, long enough for you to transfer all your knowledge, all your notes, into my memory. You're going to teach me how to use your equipment. You're going to teach me all about vitamins. You will teach me why each one is important and how much of each . . ." Carlos hesitated. "You get where I'm going with this, Hoyt? I'm going to do the presentation. And your life depends on my performance. If I do good, you go home to Lisa." He hesitated for another moment. "You can go home a rich man, Hoyt."

Hoyt turned to face him, their faces only two feet apart. "You're serious."

"Yeah, Hoyt, dead serious. What do you need to make this happen?"

In spite of himself, Hoyt chuckled at Carlos' inability to comprehend the complexity of the process. And then he decided to use it to his advantage. He spent the next few moments trying to convince Carlos that it was necessary to take him to his actual lab, but realized he wasn't making any headway.

Carlos shook his head. Clearly, he would have nothing to do with that idea. "It happens here and it happens tonight."

For a moment, Hoyt started to list in his head the items he would need. He was on the verge of stating that the task was an impossibility. For starters, Carlos would have to be on Hoyt's vitamin and mineral regimen for a month. Well, three weeks at least, but there was no need to tell Carlos that. And to make this happen out here, in a shed, not likely even if he had two months. He knew, if Carlos wanted to be the keeper of this technology, that he would subject himself to whatever Hoyt told him would be necessary to get the job done. Satisfying himself about how he'd need to play this, Hoyt began to list items he would need.

"It's too hot in here. We need to air condition this place. And we need good lighting."

Carlos acknowledged this. "You'll get a fan and a lamp."

"I need a table." Hoyt looked back into Carlos' eyes. "Some fresh clothes and a comfortable chair. Someone is going to have to go to the lab for my notes, and the neural imprinter."

Carlos was busy writing Hoyt's list but hesitated. *Maybe he can't spell neural imprinter, or he wouldn't know one if he saw it.* Hoyt pressed on. "You know, the tone machine. It's still plugged into the same place as when you were last at the lab, four months ago."

Carlos nodded.

Hoyt continued. "You'll have to bring the cords, too, and my iPad."

Carlos looked at him, as if preparing a question. "Why the iPad? You didn't use the iPad in the demonstration to me."

Hoyt fixed him with a stare. *Shut up and listen.* "If you want me to pull this off from here, I'm going to have to record all my notes onto the iPad while the toner embeds the tone that makes the memory retention possible. You are going to have to listen to my voice for hours. Can you do that?"

Carlos nodded. "What else do you need?"

Hoyt continued to rattle off his inventory. "Bring the note pads from the top drawer by the dry erase board. Go to the shelves along the back wall and grab a bottle of ascorbic acid, also choline bitartrate, resveratrol."

Carlos stopped writing and handed the pen and pad to Hoyt. He stood and returned down the driveway to get cell service. Hoyt noted that his captor was once again on the phone. When Hoyt finally finished, Carlos had returned. He handed the three pages of scribbled notes back to Carlos, who read it through, chuckling at the last item. "Sausage and pepperoni pizza. We're on a mission here, Hoyt. I'll bring us all something to eat. You worry about making this happen." Hoyt had thoughts of tricking Carlos and his crew into setting off the alarm at the lab but he had no guarantee they would get caught. Anything shy of getting the whole team arrested seemed to lead back to Lisa, and to his own demise. For now, he knew, he needed to gain Carlos' trust.

* * *

Trapped in the house, Lisa was pacing back and forth, sipping just a little too much Scotch. She was a caged animal and quickly losing her composure. She dragged one of the kitchen chairs around the house, placing it under each of the three smoke detectors Hoyt had insisted they have. She tested the one in the bedroom, the one in Hoyt's office and the one just outside the kitchen that seemed to go off every time she used the broiler. As she stepped down off the chair she lost her balance, landing on her ass. Between the liquor and the stress, getting up seemed like too much trouble. She lay there, exhausted and frustrated with her current situation and lack of a plan. She wasn't even sure what to plan for. That's when she noticed the two-by-three-foot frame outlined on the ceiling. The dreaded crawl space where she made Hoyt store the Christmas stuff and other seasonal items. Hoyt had squeezed plank after plank of plywood sheets, cut in half longways, up that tiny hole to lay as a floor so he could make use of the big space up there. She remembered him saying, "If I were five feet tall, I could live up there." She certainly could hide up there, she realized. But she had a much better idea forming in her Scotch-soaked brain.

She lay there, on her back, for the next few minutes, staring up at that small doorway, thinking through her plan. Then, struggling to her feet, she got to work.

Lisa's plan started with a cup of coffee from her trusted Keurig single-cup coffee machine. As soon as the last gulp of coffee went down, she grabbed her flashlight and went to the closet at the end of the hall. She pulled out her toolbox and the seven-foot wooden step ladder Hoyt would use to get into the attic. He would mention every time he climbed the rickety old thing that he should go to the garage to get his lighter, eight-foot aluminum step ladder, but never actually took the time or effort. Lisa dragged the clunky wooden ladder to the attic opening and cautiously began to climb. She needed to get to the third step just to reach the ten-foot ceiling and the fourth step to be able to push the attic panel and slide it aside. Step number five enabled her to peek inside and look around with the flashlight. Stabilizing herself on one of the rafters, she eased herself to the ladder's top step. She grabbed a conveniently located ceiling joist and muscled her way up.

Hoyt had done a nice job flooring his storage space. Old lamps, folding chairs and box after box lined the plywood path. Hoyt always liked to save the boxes from his purchases in case an item needed to be returned. Old computer boxes, vacuum cleaner box, tool boxes. *You name it, we have a box.* Lisa was looking for the one marked "Xmas lights." She crawled on hands and knees, sliding the flashlight along the planks. The attic was hot and by the time she found the Christmas box she was dripping sweat from her forehead. Worse by far, she was in the middle of a panic attack. She sat heavily on the two-foot-wide plywood bridge, careful not to fall off the side and into the itchy fiberglass insulation. She dared not stand; the nails that held the shingles in place penetrated almost every inch of the roof decking. But gazing at the protruding nails, she got another idea and the energy to continue. She opened the plastic bin and began to dig through its contents. A snarl of lights proved impossible to untangle in the poor light and limiting space. But more digging exposed two new boxes, still unopened, of Lisa's favorite tiny white lights. She breathed a sigh of relief, set the flashlight upright on the narrow floor and opened the first box like a kid on Christmas morning. *Rip, rip, tear,* and discard the box. She made her way back to the attic opening where an outlet was attached to the rafters. She stuck in the plug, illuminating the light rope in her hand. Years ago, Hoyt had put a basic light socket with a pull chain over the entrance, but his last time up, he'd smacked his head on it, shattering the bulb and almost catching his hair on fire. Unraveling her trail of lights along the way, Lisa crawled towards the back of the attic, as far as she could get before claustrophobia set in. She maneuvered a few boxes around, so the lights would turn around a blind corner to the right. She dropped the remaining ten feet of light rope and returned to the entrance. Before easing herself down to the ladder, she turned to look at her work. It was a pathway to her hiding place, of course. At least that's what she was hoping her captors would think.

She clumsily made her way down the ladder, almost falling twice. She made sure to leave the attic hatch open just a sliver and the ladder directly underneath.

From her toolbox, she pulled out a box of big nails that until now were simply too long for any job around the house. She took the beautiful tablecloth off her even more beautiful soft cedarwood table. She loved her cedar breakfast table. She'd had Hoyt varnish it four times to get just the finish she wanted. He'd laughed at her for getting it just the way she wanted it . . . and then covering it. She took a last loving look at her table and began to drive one big spike after another into it. At first she kept the nails, but eventually just slammed them in wherever the biggest opening was. Finally, the box was empty. Exhausted from hammering, she took a seat on the wicker bench that was also her hideaway bed. Three deep breaths later, she crawled under the table and rolled onto her back, looking up at her beautiful pincushion of nails.

Back on her feet, she put her tablecloth back over the table to conceal the nail heads.

* * *

Three hours after Hoyt surrendered his list to Carlos, Louis' truck pulled up, followed by a van. Carlos had stayed behind, just in case Hoyt remembered something else he needed. He was orchestrating this project from his new temporary office on the driveway, sending his crew to pick up whatever Hoyt demanded.

Hoyt had to give up the code to his lab's rear entrance, directing them up the back stairs to keep anyone at the neighboring businesses from asking questions. They'd left him still chained to the front of the trailer.

When they returned, the guys seemed to have their marching orders and worked like a construction crew. "Let's get that piece of shit out of there," one of the crew said, pointing to the trailer. Two guys teamed up, one on the back and one on the front, guiding the trailer to a spot just outside the shed. The lead guy talked to Hoyt as if he was part of the crew. "I need you to steer off to the side more, so we can get this stuff into the garage."

Hoyt caught Carlos' eye and pointed at his chained-up ankle. "Can I get this thing taken off?"

Carlos had peeled off his button-up dress shirt when the guys pulled up the driveway and was sweating along with his team in a white V-neck T-shirt. "Louis, chain him to the door rail so he can tell us where to put stuff." Carlos was fairly personable when his guys weren't around. But when any of them were in view, he would go out of his way for a show of power.

The first thing out of the van was an eight-foot folding table, followed by an old office chair on wheels. Hoyt had no idea where they'd gotten the chair, certainly not from his office. Paul, the big guy, came out of the passenger side with a beat-up old window fan and at least two hundred feet of extension cord. A gasoline generator was hooked up behind the shed; the extension cords were snaked into the shed and plugged into a six-outlet power station. Two matching upright lamps were carried into the garage; the guy looked at Hoyt like he was a decorator. "Where do you want these lamps?" On his second trip to the van, Paul came out with a big box full of the smaller items on Hoyt's list. Louis carried a smaller box into the garage and handed it to Carlos. "Here are the notes that you wanted." Carlos spent a few minutes leafing through the two spiral notebooks. Then he then lifted the neural transmitter. He eyed it up and down to see where the accompanying hardware plugged in, then laid it back into the box. He grabbed the iPad and turned it on to make sure Hoyt wasn't able to get an Internet connection. Carlos' guys dropped off three folding chairs before disappearing as fast as they'd showed up, leaving Hoyt with Carlos, Paul and Louis. Paul unfolded one of the chairs and plopped his ass down, wiping his forehead onto as much of his short-sleeved shirt as he could get to his head. He pulled a pack of cigarettes out of his shirt pocket and offered one to Louis.

Hoyt looked over the guys who were all sitting now. "Can I get out of these chains now?"

Surrounded by his cronies, Carlos was in thug mode. "Move the table closer to the wall and chain him to the shelf." Once chained up inside, Hoyt started to unpack the items from the box. He pulled out the iPad. Nonchalantly opening the recording app, he laid the tablet face down on the table with the microphone facing towards the trio. He laid his notebooks on top to keep it out of sight.

Carlos gave Hoyt his best tough-guy look. "Best get started. I'll be back in a few hours to check on your progress."

Hoyt had one urgent piece of business to conclude. He needed to replace the twelve-inch piece of rebar that he'd hidden between two of the trailer's planks. It had been out of reach since the trailer got moved outside. "Let me at least take a piss and smoke one of those cigarettes."

Carlos straightened up and gave Hoyt an odd look. "Funny, I didn't take you for a smoker."

Hoyt shrugged. He was just trying to give the guys as much time as possible to talk among themselves while he was outside. He hoped to record them saying something that would tip him off to their plan. "Quit about a year ago. I could really go for one now."

Carlos looked at Paul. "Give him a cigarette." Then at Louis. "You heard him. He has to take a piss. Go take your dog for a walk."

Hoyt was staring at Carlos as Louis removed the lock from the far end of his leash.

"What?" Carlos mumbled. "You got a problem?"

"No problem," Hoyt replied. "Just wonder if you realize that you're about to be the second most knowledgeable person in the world in the field of neurotransmission memory." Hoyt was hoping to feed Carlos' ego. It backfired.

Louis walked Hoyt around to the shed's side wall. He chained him to an industrial water spigot, far enough back that Louis could talk to Carlos or Paul without being heard. The addition of the noisy fan, Hoyt realized, gave the three swindlers confidence he couldn't hear their conversation.

\* \* \*

Louis spoke first. "Are we really cutting him into the deal?"

Carlos huffed out a laugh. "What do you think?" When neither guy replied, Carlos continued. "Once we're sure this really works, we'll go get Lisa. Tell her we're bringing her to see Hoyt. We lock 'em both in here and in about three days I'll be the most knowledgeable person in the world in the field of neurotransmission memory. We still have that one loose end." After waiting expectantly, his face fell, a bit disappointed that both his guys were waiting to learn what that loose end was. "Tim. Hoyt's friend Tim. He's going to have to have an accident." Carlos nodded to Louis. "Go get your dog. I have to get out of this heat."

Louis fetched Hoyt, walking him back inside, and chained him to the center rack of the industrial shelving. Hoyt walked slowly to keep the small piece of rebar from working its way out of his loose sock.

\* \* \*

"You better get started," Carlos said with a nod toward Hoyt's wish-list box.

Hoyt came right back at him. "*You* better get started. You have to get these vitamins and minerals into your system before this will work." He began to pull out bottle after bottle of his signature vitamins. As casually as he could manage, he picked up the iPad and tapped the recorder's "end" button. "Here are the items and the timeframes for taking them," he told Carlos. "Do you have a timer to remind you to take these? You're going to be popping something every few hours for the next three days so you can retain this information." Now, Hoyt was just making shit up. This was his opportunity to drug Carlos or at least swing things in his favor. Hoyt flipped through his notes. He stopped at a page about basic supplementation that he'd used about six months ago when he'd been a guest speaker at the local college. "Start reading this section of my notes to get an idea of the importance of nutrients and neural transmission. While you review that, I'll look for your first lesson."

Hoyt used this distraction to accomplish two important goals. First, he retrieved the rebar from his sock and slipped it into the box while pretending to fuss with its contents. Next, he plugged his headset into the iPad and started to play back the recording of the three thugs' discussion when he'd been out of earshot outside. He tried not to react as he listened to Carlos' plan to kill them all. Carlos intended to let him, Lisa and Tim rot together, right here in the storage shed.

Hoyt turned off the recording and addressed Carlos. "We have a few problems."

"What?" Carlos said as he closed the notebook, obviously bored with the material.

"The battery in the transmitter is never going to last long enough for all this information. Once the battery gets weak, the tone slows down and retention is affected. You're going to have to send two guys back to the lab to get my back-up battery and the charging station."

Carlos' raised-eyebrow look meant "please elaborate."

"The backup battery is in the charging station. The charging station is in the biohazard room."

Carlos' head was wagging back and forth, his body language asking, "Why?"

"That's where I do most of my recording. It's no big deal. Here is what you have to do." Hoyt explained how the sensor card would be hanging on a hook just outside the door marked "Biohazard Authorized Personnel Only."

All three men were paying attention. Carlos slid one of Hoyt's notebooks to Paul. "Take notes, dipshit."

Hoyt continued. "Once you're in, you have thirty seconds to punch in the code on the keypad inside. The code is 2436 'pound.'"

Carlos looked to make sure Paul included the hashtag.

"Here is the reason you both need to go." Hoyt waited for eye contact from Paul and Louis. "Once you hit the code, you will send an alert to our security folks. The phone on the wall will ring and they will want to hear my voice. If I don't pick up the phone, they will send someone over to make sure someone isn't raiding the drugs. Security will be there in three minutes."

Paul spoke up first. "So, we have three minutes to get your battery thing and get out? That's too risky." Hoyt put up his index finger, indicating that there was more.

"Especially since the charger is in my locker. That's why we need you both to go. There is a way to beat the system." Hoyt stood up to better demonstrate. "Let's say Paul uses the card scanner to get in and heads right to my locker in the back of the room. Louis goes right for the key pad and punches in the code. But . . . when you hit the pound key," Hoyt hesitated for effect, looking directly at Louis, "don't release it. It's programmed to shut off the alarm when you push it in, and it triggers the call to security when you release it. Like I said, the battery charger is in my locker. The code is also 2436. As long as Louis holds the pound key in, you have all the time you need. Once you have what you came for, get out of there. Three minutes is plenty of time to get down the back stairs and into your car." None of this was true, but Hoyt's plan was to get both men completely inside the Biohazard room.

Hoyt went silent. It was like one of those heavy sales-training pitches where they teach you that the first one to talk loses.

Carlos lost. "Sounds doable. You know your life depends on it. Right?"

Hoyt knew Carlos had already mentally spent the ten million dollars. He wasn't going to let a three-minute window stop him from collecting.

"Anything else I need to know?" Carlos asked.

Hoyt was lying up a storm; he decided to take it to the next level.

"Yes, you're going to need to pick up some Bayer aspirin to thin your blood."

Carlos tilted his head upward, silently asking for an explanation.

Hoyt acknowledged him. "To thin your blood."

Carlos wanted more.

"To break the blood barrier to your brain easier."

Carlos pretended to understand. "What else?"

Hoyt continued thinking off the cuff. "You're going to need Viagra." Paul and Louis caught each other's eyes and snickered like a couple of school kids.

"I don't need Viagra," Carlos said, a hint of anger in his voice.

"Well, then, you'd better plan on bringing a treadmill and running the whole time you're listening to the recording."

Again, Carlos raised his eyebrow.

"We have to get your heart rate up to 120. Were you paying attention at all during my presentation four months ago?" In reality, Hoyt did want him on aspirin, but only so he would bleed out faster if opportunity allowed cutting or stabbing him with the rebar. The Viagra would get Carlos' blood pumping, also helping to assure a quick demise. Hoyt had actually used Viagra in the early stages of testing. He'd had to find a safe way to keep his heart rate up without the constant running. Viagra did the trick, but the bulge in his pants often lasted longer than the sessions. Lisa had often been the beneficiary of those studies. But ultimately, he had found a better system.

Hoyt had recently synthesized a concoction that sent the perfect ratio of blood to his head and not his penis. But, of course, he had no need to share this discovery with Carlos. Hoyt figured the Viagra's signature effects would be one more distraction for Carlos to deal with. As a parting gift, he gave Carlos eight small pills from an unmarked bottle. "Take two of these, every hour for the next four hours and meet me back here at sunrise. Drink a lot of water. This will open up capillaries in your brain. If you feel a little dizzy, sit down and relax for a moment. You might feel a little like you smoked a joint. It will pass quickly." The pills had actually been prescribed for Hoyt's occasional constipation and were sure to give Carlos major diarrhea. That would be sweet revenge, Hoyt reflected, after what he'd just been through himself. "Take the Viagra first thing in the morning with a cup of coffee and be ready to amaze yourself." Hoyt chuckled inside. *More like, be ready to shit yourself with a boner.*

Carlos bought it, hook, line and sinker. Before leaving, he gave his guys some last-minute instructions. "Wait till dusk. Call me as soon as you have the charging station. Apparently, I need to get a watch with a timer."

"You're going to need sleep, too," Hoyt added.

This time, when they locked Hoyt into the unit, he had light and a fan. He was also glad they had stacked some of the old rotted planks in the back of the shed. They'd also agreed to leave one of the bigger slivers of wood under the door by the fan to circulate some air from outside. It wasn't much, but the two-inch gap, a fan and some light were more than he'd had before. As soon as he was sure both vehicles were gone, he reached into the bottom of the box to retrieve his precious foot-long piece of rebar. He slid it into one of the links that pressed against the metal shelf. He twisted with all the strength he had. He was able to bend the link but not to break it. He found a dirty rag on the shelf and wrapped it around the rebar's sharp edge. He wrapped his sweatshirt around the other end. With a hand at each end, he twisted back and forth, hoping the link would give way before his tender, white-collar skin did. Five long minutes later, he was free. Free, at least, from the shelf. He was still locked in a storage shed with twelve feet of chain attached to his ankle

# Chapter 6 - Biohazard

All this time, Tim was busy making himself crazy. He had led a fairly straightforward life. Knowing that people were following him, people with guns, took him to new mental depths. He had never been shot at, let alone shot. For that matter, he had only fired a gun once. He drove to his work to switch out the car that had been "made" with his non-descript work vehicle, and to arm himself with the Taser that Hoyt had sent to him. Before leaving the house, he changed into a different coat and put on his tattered Cubs baseball cap. He was hoping to go back to the house again to get his dog. If the men were watching the place, he would keep tabs on them from his battered old station wagon. He used the junker for delivering greasy printer components to the repair shop. The shocks were shot, leaving the car to bounce after every bump. The brakes were just starting to grind whenever the car came to a complete stop. He'd fought with the idea of fixing up the junker but by now he was resigned to just driving it till it fell apart.

Before starting, he made sure his phone was handy and had enough charge to last the night; his junker didn't have a charging port. The battery indicator read 65 percent. It would have to do. He and Lisa had agreed to text one another every fifteen minutes to make sure they were both okay. They would alternate texts. First Tim to Lisa, then Lisa to Tim.

On his way back to his house the phone beeped. He figured it was Lisa and ignored it for the moment. He had his eyes on his house. He inched up closer, trying to make out whether it was still under surveillance. He tugged on his baseball cap, keeping his hand on the visor to block his face. He prepared to respond to Lisa to let her know he was about to go into the house when he noticed the text wasn't from her. It read, "in trouble, you and Lisa in danger." Tim didn't recognize the number but figured it must be Hoyt.

He hesitated. "This you Hoyt?" *Send.*

Five long minutes passed. He wanted to call Lisa but first had to make sure he'd really heard from Hoyt. Finally, a second text came through. "Tenth grade Ms. Elliot." Tim smiled. He knew Hoyt was referring to their English teacher from tenth grade. She'd been a hottie. They'd both had a crush on her.

\* \* \*

Hoyt had used the shovel to pry up the door enough to slide one of the long trailer planks underneath. He would type out his text message, hit *send* and place the iPad on the plank, sliding it out as far as he could to pick up a signal. He wished he had a rubber band or tape to secure the iPad so it wouldn't slip off the plank. He would slide the plank out as far as he could, then lift the mail slot and wait to hear the *ping* of transmission. He would have to leave the iPad fully extended to receive a response. The setup wasn't good, but it was all he had.

\* \* \*

"Where are you? Can I call?" Tim typed. *Send.*

Tim stared at the phone waiting for a response that didn't come. He was pretty sure it was Hoyt. Unless they are torturing him or something. Maybe they told him to come up with something personal just to get info from me. Tim continued to make himself nuts. "They're probably homing in on my location now," he thought out loud. Finally the phone pinged again.

"Text only. iPad
Trapped in storage shed.
2 bad guys going to my lab at dusk.
Hide. When they enter
Biohazard room make sure
door closes. Will lock in
Hurry, then come get me"

Tim looked at his watch. 6:14. Dusk is a relative term. *It starts to get dark about 7:00 this time of year.* Tim had to put his plans of rescuing Max on hold.

\* \* \*

Lisa had dozed off under her table full of nails. Checking her phone, she saw that Tim hadn't texted her in forty-five minutes. She scooched her way out from under the table and stood. She was dizzy from lack of food and an overabundance of fine whisky. She quickly tapped a text to Tim, "You okay" and laid the phone on the table. She pulled open the refrigerator and stared at its contents. The phone pinged but she didn't read it. The sound of the ping was comfort enough for the moment. Nothing in the fridge looked enticing. Some scrambled eggs sounded good, but only if someone else cooked them. A piece of bread with peanut butter would have to do. She slapped a wad of peanut butter on a slice of white and folded it in half. She changed out the used brew cup in her

Keurig and inserted a fresh one. When her coffee was ready, she gathered it up along with her peanut butter and bread taco and headed back to the table. Sitting on her hideaway bench, she took a huge bite and prepared to reply to whatever text Tim sent.

"Hoyt is okay. Trapped in some shed.
We have plan. Here is his tablet number
727-504-3457 text only. Say hi"

Lisa read the text five times before she comprehended.

"!!!!! How okay if still trapped?
What plan? Be careful.
Should I hide?"

\* \* \*

Tim was rolling through stop signs and putting his beater station wagon to the test as he sped to Hoyt's lab, hoping to get there before his opponents. He had been to the lab at least a dozen times over the fifteen years that Hoyt owned it. He parked the junky old car down the street and took the Taser out of the glovebox. He studied it. It was identical to the one Hoyt had given to Lisa. *He must have suspected that he—and we—were in danger.*

Hoyt knew Tim wasn't a gun guy. Guns scared him. He'd once pulled the trigger on a shotgun as a young man when a friend of a friend talked him into going pig hunting. He never expected to pull the trigger, but the damn pig ran right across his path. "Shoot him. Shoot him!" He aimed and shot; the blast kicked his shoulder back and left his ear ringing for hours. He missed the pig. At least that's what he always told himself.

He shook the memory from his mind and pressed the trigger of his Taser, releasing a commanding *zap*. He shuddered at the thought of actually Tasing someone. "This is a stealth mission. This is going to work," he said, just loud enough to convince himself. He hoped.

He went to the back of the building and punched in the code to the back door. He hurried up the stairs, punching in the same code for door number two. Hoyt had used the same code for as long as he'd owned the place.

When Tim entered the second door, it was dark. He felt the inside wall, hoping to find the light switch. He groped his way around four switches, pondering whether he should turn any of them on. He checked his watch. 6:55 p.m. He decided to leave the lights off and make his way back using the LED flashlight built into his modest Taser. The lab was basically a giant rectangle. Lab equipment, shiny tables and work stations on the left and three offices on the right. The Biohazard room was straight back all the way at the end of the laboratory. He shined the substandard torch's light on the door at the lab's far end. The flashlight was too weak to illuminate the distant door, but as he got closer he was able to read the "WARNING BIOHAZARD" sign. A pull on the doorknob confirmed it was locked. He worried that Hoyt might have overlooked this detail. He smiled and nodded his head, thinking, *We're talking about Hoyt.* Tim imagined the two thugs coming into this room. All lights would be on, so Tim would have to surprise them and close the bio room door before they heard him or saw him. What if one waited outside? He imagined Tasing one and locking in the other. He settled into the office closest to the biohazard room. He was a good twenty steps away but was able to see the bio door if he kept the office door open just an inch or two.

His phone pinged. And his heart began to race. *No texting! Turn off your phone, you idiot! You know better.* As he read Lisa's text, which said, "Hoyt is at old Dearborn Industrial building," Tim heard the ground floor door open. Muffled voices came up the stairwell. He texted back, "shhhhhhh danger." Lisa apparently got the message; her communications stopped. When the second door opened, Tim could hear the two men clear as day.

"Turn on the lights, Louis," one of the voices said.

"All of 'em?"

"Yeah, all of them."

As the sections of the lab lit up, Tim felt visible, and vulnerable. He closed the office door all but a sliver and slid down onto his knees. He wanted to lie on the floor all army-man style but was afraid getting into position would make too much noise.

"Put something in front of the door just in case we set off an alarm. I don't want to get locked in here." Best Tim could tell, the big, beefy guy who had spoken was talking about the entry door and not the bio room. All the same, Tim stayed on alert.

A second, much thinner man was looking around. *Must be the one he called "Louis."*

"The key is supposed to be hanging up in the back, by the door," the big guy said.

As the steps got closer and the voices got louder, Tim closed the office door even more.

"Paul, is this it?" Louis lifted the lanyard off the hook and held it in front of the bio room's doorknob. The beep startled Louis; he must not have expected it to work from a foot away. They two thugs looked at each other with wide eyes, realizing the thirty-second timer had started.

Tim knew from Hoyt's texts that the intruders had only thirty seconds to get inside the bio room and tap the PIN code into the pad. "Don't let go of the 'pound' key till I say!" he heard the big guy, Paul, reminded his lanky companion as he bolted to the back of the room. Tim's heart was pounding out of his chest. His hands were wet and clammy. Salty sweat dripped into eyes; wiping it from his eyes, he almost Tased himself. Paul made his way to the back of the bio room like a bull in a china shop. "I don't see a locker." His voice was tense and loud. Louis was using one hand to hold the door open, Tim could see, stretching his other arm to keep one finger on the "pound" button.

*Now!* Tim told himself. *Now!* He stood and opened the office door. Before getting halfway through, he slipped on a puddle of his own sweat, cracking his knee on the lab floor. His Taser hit the tile and spun off towards the bio door. Paul was noisily tossing things around in the back of the biohazard room, but Louis must have heard a noise from outside. By the time he stuck his head through the door opening, Tim had crawled halfway to him. Just before he reached the Taser, he looked up to meet eyes with Louis. Tim had to decide: *Go for the door or the Taser?* There wasn't time for both. Louis looked back at Paul and then at the pad on the wall.

Tim knew what must be going through the guy's head: if he went for his gun, he would have to either let go of the door or release the "pound" key that sets off the alarm. Tim slammed into the door, trying to get a good grip on the knob with his sweaty hands. He started to pull before he was able to get good footing. Louis abandoned the keypad, slid the fingers of both hands between the door and its frame and started to pull. Paul was on his way back to the door, a crazy look in his eyes. If he made it, the tug of war was going to go the wrong way. Tim suddenly switched momentum from pull to push and rammed the heavy door into Louis' face. He quickly pulled back, slamming Louis' fingers against the frame. Louis screamed profanities and pulled out his mashed fingers. Tim pulled the door shut moments before Paul arrived to help. He held the door handle as tight as he could, not convinced the door was locked. Louis was still cursing up a storm and screaming how he was "gonna kill that mother fucker!"

"Move!" Paul shoved Louis aside and yanked back and forth on the door with all his might. Tim slid to the ground, his back to the door and hands over his ears, knowing that if the door didn't hold, he was a dead man. His Taser was just out of reach. It seemed to be laughing at him. When Paul finally let up, Tim lunged for his Taser, grabbed it and stood. He took two deep breaths to try to calm himself. The bio room was suddenly quiet. Too quiet. A heavy blow smashed against the door's six-inch square peep window. A second and a third smash finally cracked the thick glass. "Get back!" Paul's voice warned Louis. *BANG!* A bullet zipped through the safety glass and right past Tim's head. He dived to the floor and scooted up to the door again, this time with Taser in hand, sitting with his back against the door frame. Paul used the gun butt to break out the rest of the small window. His fat face pushed up against the opening. "Where are you, you little prick?" Apparently spotting Tim's feet, he stretched so his eye was at the top of the window, trying to make out more of Tim's body. That gave Tim a close-up view of one bugged-out eye, the white at the top and a dark blue, almost purple, iris at the bottom. The eye suddenly backed away and a hairy arm with a gun protruded through the opening. Another bang and another near miss, right into the floor between Tim's legs. Tim jammed the zapping Taser upward against Paul's wrist, causing him to fire two more rounds before dropping the gun and withdrawing his arm. Tim dropped his Taser and shuffled across the floor, clumsily scooping up the gun. Paul had his eye back up to the opening screaming profanities at Tim.

Tim held the gun with both hands, shakily pointing it at Paul.

"You're not gonna shoot anybody, you little worm."

*Oh, I'm not, am I?* Tim steadied his hands and squeezed the trigger. His shot went into the steel door, backing Paul up. Tim quickly approached the window opening. He fired a second shot through the gap, breaking some glass beakers and puncturing the refrigerator at the room's far end. The two men were crouched there in defensive positions. Tim stuck his arm through the window, struggling to keep one and then the other man in sight. This wasn't easy, with his own arm blocking most of the view through the little opening. Paul must have seen this; he relaxed and started to stand. Tim aimed the gun right at his head. "Don't make me shoot you!"

Paul was massaging his wrist where the Taser had zapped him. "It's a six shooter," he laughed. "You're out of bullets."

Tim pulled his arm out of the little window and backed away.

This time it was Louis who stuck his head up to the window. "You're a dead man," he said softly, shaking his head. "You're a dead man. You hear me? A dead man." This time, he was yelling and spitting.

Tim backed up to one of the lab tables and sat on it, the empty gun in his hand. He laid the revolver on the table and bent over to retrieve his Taser.

He knew they had the card that opened the door in there with them. It was only a matter of time before they figured out they could dangle it on its lanyard through the window and gain their freedom.

As Tim scanned the office for something to cover the card-reading sensor, Louis kept poking his face up to the window, reminding him how he's a dead man.

"C'mere, I just want to talk to you." The tone in Louis's voice clearly meant, "If I could just get my hands on you, I would pull you through this little hole and beat you to a pulp." Tim found an Xacto knife and with one hand began scratching up the face of the sensor. With the other, he kept the Taser ready, zapping at the window anytime Louis got close. Then it dawned on him. Dropping the knife, he held the Taser half an inch from the sensor and zapped away. A smile of contentment and pride filled his face. A tiny wisp of smoke rose from the fried sensor. He was tempted to ask the guys for the card just so he could test his work.

He heard Paul's voice through the window, evidently on the phone. "Uh, we ran into a problem." Tim wanted to hear the rest of this conversation but knew he'd better get out before Paul and Louis found a way to bust down the door or unhinge it from the inside. He also needed to get out before someone else showed up. Then he noticed a smoke-colored plastic wall pocket hanging just outside the biohazard room. In it were a file and a spiral notebook. Fishing around in his pocket, he found Hoyt's cell phone. Tim dialed his own number from Hoyt's phone before slipping it into the hanging pocket. With the line open, he'd be able to hear anything Paul and Louis said, assuming they said it loud enough. Tim stuffed the gun into the rear of his pants, by now feeling pretty gangster. He pulled his Taser back out of his pocket and headed for the door, his phone to his ear. As he slipped out of the lab, he flipped off all the lights, just to further hinder their escape attempt.

Tim was able to make out Louis' voice. "Get out of the way; my arms are longer than yours."

Paul was finishing up his phone conversation. "He snuck up on us with a Taser."

After some silence, Louis' voice came through, loud and clear. "He blocked it with something." Louis' attempts to get the shoe off the doorknob made it hard to hear Paul.

"How would he know we were coming here? . . . Yeah. Okay." With that, Paul's phone call ended. "Louis, relax. He's sending the cops to get us out." *The cops.* Suddenly Tim realized Lisa hadn't been so paranoid after all. After a moment, he heard Paul tell his partner something else important. "Carlos is really pissed off."

Louis interrupted. "It's not our fault. He came out of nowhere!" Some indistinct noises followed. *Did I hear a refrigerator door closing?* And something seemed to have fallen with a thud. Tim flipped the phone to his left ear so he could use his right hand to fish his keys out of his pocket. As he started the car, cell phone glued to his ear, he finally heard Louis ask the question he wanted to hear. "What is Carlos planning to do?"

\* \* \*

Back at the storage shed, Hoyt was still working on his escape. Systematically, he used the shovel to pry up the door an inch or two at a time and then shoved in a plank to maintain his progress. Pry, shove; pry, shove. With every board he added, the prying got harder. The left side of the door, with the lock, stood firm but Hoyt had the right side up to a six-inch gap. He would need one more board, maybe two, to be able to slither under the door. He secured another board but while attempting to get enough space for the last one, he broke the shovel. The planks from the trailer bed were mostly rotted. They were good for jamming under the door but not strong enough to pry. Hoyt had to go for it. By now, he figured, Paul and Louis were locked in the lab. Or, for all he knew, Tim was dead. He slid the iPad outside and lay down on his back, turning his head sideways so he could poke it through to the other side. The sun was just setting; Hoyt probably had twenty minutes before complete darkness. The opening to the right of the rotted planks was now about eight inches at the far end, steadily less with every foot closer to the door's locked side. His stack of rotted planks left him a usable opening only about two feet wide. With his head outside and his body still stuck inside, he began to panic. He inched his way until his chest jammed against the metal door and simply couldn't force his rib cage through the opening. He twisted his head and wormed his way back onto the shed.

He needed leverage from the inside. The metal shelves were about eight feet back. He lined up one of the shorter, broken planks against the shelf, turned on edge and parallel with the door. This gave him a firm surface to press his feet against. He twisted his head and slid under the opening. Again he wormed his way under, and again his chest got stuck. He bent his knees and, with his heels, felt for the resistance of the planks. He took a shallow breath and then, pushing hard against the planks, released all of his air. *Pop.* It worked! He did an upside-down army crawl, stopping only for a moment to clear his belt buckle, and he was free. He carried the iPad to the middle of the driveway, where it started to ping. He quickly caught up on the barrage of messages Tim and Lisa had sent him.

"Guys are trapped! Not sure
for how long. Cops in on it.
Going to get them out.
Really mad at me. Going to
take it out on you. Where are
you? I will come get you.
Lisa is hiding.
You okay?"

Hoyt was finally able to reply.

"Busted out! Meet me at
my house."

Hoyt was angry at himself for not figuring out sooner where he was. He pressed the Uber app and saw an available car about eight minutes away. He gathered up his twelve-foot chain and used the iPad for a light. Two minutes after he requested Uber service, a car slowed down to turn into the long driveway. Hoyt looked at the iPad screen. His driver was still five minutes away. He pressed the light of the tablet to his chest and ducked behind one of the cement pillar bases from which tall electrical towers rose.

A dark SUV sped up the driveway, skidding to a stop just before the door. Carlos got out of the car and got a look at the light coming out under the one corner. "Son of a . . ." He didn't finish the sentence. He followed the trail of scuffed gravel the chain had made about twenty steps up the driveway, looking left and then right. He marched back to the vehicle, got in and slammed the door. The tires spit stones everywhere as he raced back to the road. Hoyt was praying that Carlos would leave before his Uber ride showed up. *Hallelujah!* The moment Carlos' taillights vanished, a new set of headlights appeared. The Uber driver gave Hoyt a strange look as he climbed into the front seat with his filthy outfit, iPad and armful of chain. "I need to use your phone."

"Sorry dude, I don't–"

Hoyt interrupted him. "Call the fuckin' police. No, give me the phone." During one of Hoyt's early Viagra-induced listening sessions, he had memorized his entire contact list. All 612 phone numbers, home addresses and email addresses. He decided that his first call should be to Tim.

# Chapter 7 - The Sting

Thanks to Hoyt's perfectly placed cell phone, Tim had been listening in to everything Louis and Paul were saying. When another call came in, he let the phone ring seven times before deciding to answer. He put the first call on hold to be sure he didn't lose the connection, and picked up the new call without saying a word.

"It's me," the familiar voice came out of the phone.

"Hoyt! Holy shit!" Tim said. "The two cops are on their way to your lab." Tim spastically rattled off some of the conversation he had overhead.

Hoyt cut him off mid-sentence, instructing Tim to hurry to the police station.

"But the cops are in on it," Tim insisted.

Based on the conversation he'd been able to overhear, Hoyt explained, he was pretty sure Cleveland and Melbern were the only cops in on the scam. With them out of the station, Hoyt said, he hoped the rest of the department was on the up and up.

* * *

When Tim got to the station, he insisted on talking to Sergeant Jenkins. It took some insisting, but he was able to get to the sergeant. As Jenkins approached him, a call came over one of the officers' shoulder radios. "This is Officer Cleveland. We're going to respond to a four-fifteen in the warehouse district."

The officer responded, "Are you calling for backup?"

The line was silent for a moment before Cleveland replied. "No, just an FYI."

Sergeant Jenkins looked past Tim and addressed his dispatcher. "Did you get a call for a disturbance in the warehouse district?"

The dispatcher shook her head and raised an eyebrow.

Jenkins held up a finger to Tim and addressed his dispatcher again. "Ask them, 'Where in the warehouse district?'"

An even longer pause was followed by a rushed response from Officer Cleveland. "There is an alarm going off at that vitamin warehouse . . . I'm sure it's nothing."

Tim, now frantic, rudely interrupted Jenkins' inquiry. "That's why I'm here!" he said in a voice loud enough to turn most of the heads in the precinct. "Is there somewhere that we can talk privately? . . . Right now!"

Jenkins picked up a notebook, and motioned for Tim to follow him back into one of the holding rooms.

The moment the door to the holding room closed Tim started talking a hundred miles an hour. "Your officers are in on it!" he blurted. "They're working with the guys that took Hoyt!" "Whoa, slow down ... in on what?" said Jenkins motioning for Tim to calm down with a pulsing hand motion. Tim's voice was a high pitch, nearly a squeal. "They're trying to kill us!" Jenkins motioned for Tim to sit down. "That's a very strong accusation. What evidence do you have?" Jenkins put his hands on his hips and looked at Tim with a raised eyebrow. Tim obliged, still standing. "We are about to hear to a conversation between your officers and the two people robbing the place." Tim held his phone out, between himself and the sergeant and repeated himself, a bit louder, "Between your officers Cleveland and Melbern and the two thugs they're working with. They don't know that we can hear them. They are clearly planning to kill me and my friends, Lisa and Hoyt."

Jenkins motioned for Tim to let him listen to the conversation. Tim laid the phone on the table and tapped the speaker button.

His timing was perfect; Tim heard the two officers just announcing themselves as they entered the lab.

"We're back here." It was Louis' voice, apparently still yelling through the small broken window. His voice came loud and clear over the phone in the quiet interrogation room.

A distant voice responded. "Couple of goddamn morons."

Paul was next to speak. "Just open the damn door."

Jenkins recognized the next speaker as officer Melbern. "What do you think, Cleveland? Should we let them out?" There it was. He said her name. Tim looked up at Sergeant Jenkins for confirmation.

Jenkins waved at Tim to keep quiet so he could keep listening. The sergeant softly asked, "They can't hear us, can they?"

Tim shook his head. "Nope."

The conversation they'd picked up on Tim's improvised bug went on. "Carlos went to get Lisa," Paul said. "He's going to lock her up with Hoyt and we're all supposed find this loose cannon, Tim."

Tim looked at the sergeant and pointed to himself, as if the sergeant couldn't figure that out that he was Tim.

He got up and called in two of his veteran cops. "We have a situation. Cleveland and Melbern seem to have gone off the reservation. I'm gonna need you to take Adams and Labont with you. They're at this address, but I'm not sure I can keep 'em there for long. I need for you to surprise them, disarm them, and bring them in for questioning. No shooting."

Officer Guble was first to speak up. "What did I tell you about Cleveland? She's been squirrelly all month."

His partner nodded as he pulled out his pistol and checked the bullet count.

"Got to keep them all in the lab, somehow," Jenkins said. "How long is it going to take them to get out of the room?"

Tim shrugged. "Not sure. It's an industrial door. It opens inward, so they weren't able to bust it down from inside. I messed up the door sensor pretty bad, but your guys might be able to bust in the door from the outside."

Jenkins was nodding his head, only half listening. Suddenly his eyes lit up and he motioned for Tim to be silent. He radioed in to Officer Cleveland, asking her for an update.

"All good here."

Jenkins responded, "Good, 'cause we got another situation in that neck of the woods. Go to the Union Street housing projects." Tim knew the lab and the projects were only half a mile or so apart; he guessed the sergeant knew this, too. "I need you to cruise the area for a while. We got a call that there's a coyote running around, rattling the neighborhood. If you locate it, just call me back and we'll dispatch our friends at Animal Control." Tim could see what Sergeant Jenkins was doing: he wanted to put his two misguided officers at ease, give them an excuse to relax. Jenkins' last request would give them at least a half hour of cover to wrap up at the lab without being missed, and that's exactly what Jenkins was counting on.

Officer Cleveland answered the sergeant with a crisp "ten-four" and turned off her com.

But through Tim's phone, he and Jenkins could still hear as Melbern laughed. "We already got a couple of coyotes that got caught in a trap. Maybe we should call Animal Control for you guys." The two cops were clearly close to the bio hazard door and Paul and Louis had to be huddled just inside. The phone tucked away in the hanging wall file made their damning conversation easy to hear.

As they listened, Tim and Jenkins learned that the sensor was in fact fried. Their overheard comments made it obvious the two cops were looking around the lab for a while until Cleveland said she would have to go to the car for a crowbar. Using a back channel, Jenkins informed the four officers who were nearly there that she would be coming out of the lab's back door. This would be their chance to secure her, leaving only Melbern upstairs, along with the two criminals who were already locked up. The patrol officers decided it would be best if one car stayed just out of sight. Jenkins OK'd this plan.

\* \* \*

The other car eased its way up to Officer Cleveland while she was searching her trunk for the crowbar. Officer Labont put the window down and nonchalantly asked with a grin, "Any sign of that big bad wolf that's causing a ruckus with the neighbors?"

Cleveland had the crowbar in her hands and was caught off guard, but reacted calmly. "Yeah, he was just here."

Labont tilted his head up and asked, "So, you're gonna fight him with a crowbar?"

Cleveland rolled right back. "Well, I'm not gonna shoot the little guy. He's just a pup."

Officer Adams was already out of the passenger seat, acting as if he needed a stretch. He knew as long as she had her hands on the crowbar she didn't have either of them free to go for her gun. Labont put the car in park and got out.

Cleveland looked at the both of them and snapped. "What the fuck, did the Sarge send the whole precinct to capture a coyote?"

Adams gently pulled out his gun and replied, "Fraid not, Cleveland. He wants us to bring you in. Not gonna give us trouble, are you?"

Officer Melbern was upstairs, wandering around the lab like a kid, picking up beakers and bottles. When the door opened he figured it was Cleveland coming back with the crowbar and didn't even turn around. It had been twelve years since he'd last drawn his gun. He was all mouth. The patrol cops didn't expect him to be a problem, and he wasn't. They put Paul and Officer Cleveland in one patrol car and put Louis and Officer Melbern in another to keep the two cops from collaborating.

\* \* \*

In the confusion of Sergeant Jenkins' plot to bring in two of his own, Tim got a text from Hoyt and quietly made his way out of the station.

"Here at the house.
Where are you?"

\* \* \*

Hoyt had the Uber driver drop him off a few doors down. In the shadows the street lights cast, he saw a repair van was parked in the street with two guys in it. Another string of texts came in from Tim.

"Almost there. Caught more
bad guys. I'm in my ugly
brown station wagon"

Hoyt responded.

"Good job but more
bad guys here. I have
an idea."

* * *

Before either was able to type another text, a black Escalade zipped past Tim, sped down the street and pulled into Hoyt's driveway. The man who got out, Tim now knew, was Carlos. He didn't bother turning off the car. The headlights were aimed right at the front door. He stomped with angry purpose to the van's passenger side and yelled into the window, loud enough for Tim to hear. "Open the goddamn front door," he bellowed, pointing to the house.

A guy hustled out of the van and slid open the side door to grab his screw gun. Carlos looked at the driver. "You keep watch." His accomplice left the side door open and hustled to catch up to Carlos, who was making a bee-line for the house.

* * *

Hoyt and Lisa had already been texting. She was nicely tucked away in the breakfast nook bench. She'd told him about her attic plan but he'd said it was a long shot and a stall tactic at best. When she heard the drilling at the front door her heart started to pound at double speed. By the fourth long screw the drill was struggling to finish the job.

Faintly, from outside, she heard somebody say, "I'm going to have to get another battery."

A second voice said, "Give it to me." The groan of an overloaded electric motor, squeezing every drop of juice out of its battery, joined with the sounds of grunts, like somebody exerting a good bit of muscle force, too. The screws that held the door shut must have been removed by now, Lisa realized. But she'd had the presence of mind to set the deadbolt.

\* \* \*

Carlos was fit to be tied. He'd been taking all the meds that Hoyt had prescribed; he was nauseated and dizzy. "Break this door down or I'm gonna start shooting shit." The man, who Carlos knew only as Daz, backed up and gave the door a good hearty kick at about doorknob height. The door trim splintered, but the bolt held. This time, anyway. A good strong body check finished the job.

Both men entered like a couple of raptors looking for prey. Carlos spotted the ladder and gave the ceiling a quick look but continued to scan the room for Lisa. "Check the bedrooms." Carlos picked through the contents of Lisa's purse, still sprawled on the kitchen counter. "I know you're in here, Lisa." What he didn't know was that she was so close she could see the crease in his pants through the wicker bench's tiny holes. "We did it!" He tried to sound excited. "We're done. I can take you to see Hoyt now."

Daz came back from his search of the two bedrooms. "Nobody here."

Carlos looked suspiciously at the ladder and nudged his head upward, indicating where he wanted Daz to go.

Daz repositioned the ladder a couple of inches and locked in the metal elbows. He cautiously took the first two steps, pushed up and slid aside the wooden hatch. He hesitated for just a moment before poking his head up inside. He took a step back down and met Carlos' eyes. He nodded his head. "She's up there."

Carlos barked the next order. "Go get her!" Carlos steadied the ladder as Daz took the last two steps and, with a grunt, hoisted himself through the opening. From below, Carlos could see the glow of light coming from the opening.

Carlos couldn't help climbing up himself to see what his henchman was doing. Daz was moving the Christmas lights so as not to kneel on them during his crawl. Other than the brightly lit path, the attic was full of dark corners and a million shadows. Daz moved slowly and cautiously.

With just his head poked into the attic, Carlos felt a significant difference in temperature. "Lisa, c'mon out of there," Carlos called. "It's over. Just like I told you. Three days and now we're all going to be rich."

Daz momentarily halted his crawl to cock an ear and listen. He continued when there was no response. "Really, Lisa? You're going to make me come get you?"

Both men were silent for another moment and then Carlos barked, "Go get her."

Carlos dropped down two steps, back into the cooler air, and wiped the sweat that was already accumulating on his forehead. When he stepped off the ladder's bottom rung, he gave one last look around the living room before returning to the breakfast table to wait. He slid the table out just enough to get easy access to the wicker bench. He eased out his pistol and laid it on the table.

* * *

Lisa tightened her grip on the half scissors and the Taser. This was it. By now, thanks to Hoyt's text messages, she knew the man sitting above her was named Carlos. Any moment now, he would lift the seat cover and the horror would begin. Hoyt had told her of Carlos' plan to lock them both up at the shed. She knew Carlos was here to reunite her with her husband, but only so they could die together. She was ready to fight with everything she had.

Tim and Hoyt had devised a plan to distract the man who had stayed back in the van. They needed to take him out of the picture, so they could hide just outside the front door and ambush Carlos as he left the house. The Escalade's headlights were still pointing right at the front door and would now work to their advantage, blinding Carlos as he came out of the house. Tim still had Paul's gun; only he knew it didn't have any bullets left in it. Hoyt was still toting around his twelve-foot ankle chain. Hoyt approached the van from the rear, the chain in his hand. Except for the four feet of links that dangled down to his right ankle, the remaining eight feet were awkwardly wrapped around his arm. The van's sliding door was open and its dome light on, giving them the advantage of great visibility into the van, where the driver would have trouble seeing anything in the surrounding darkness.

Hoyt spoke up as soon as he was in visual range of the man in the front seat. "Hey buddy, you have bolt cutters in here?" The man looked Hoyt up and down but before he could react, Tim slammed the pistol butt against the driver's side window, spraying the driver with glass shards and forcing him into a fetal position. Hoyt was impressed with Tim's gangster-like actions.

"Get out of the van," commanded Tim, who followed him with the gun pointed right at his head. "Get my friend out of those chains. NOW!" The man took pains to cooperate; maybe he could tell from Tim's shaking hand just how nervous he was. The man was careful to keep his hands in view. Tim added a second sweaty hand to steady the gun.

The man slowly faced Tim and reassured him, "No trouble from me. I'm just the driver." He opened a toolbox and slowly lifted the top tray.

"Nothing stupid, buddy. I'll blow your head off." Tim was trying to sound tough, but his voice was cracking. He was almost as impatient as Hoyt, who he knew wanted the chains off quickly so he could go save Lisa. The driver kept an eye on Tim's trigger finger, noting that his hands were getting shakier by the moment. The man quickly pulled out a pair of bolt cutters. Hoyt lifted his chained ankle onto the van's floor. Tim assessed his friend's condition. Hair unruly, three-day growth of beard, and distinct body odor. Shirtless, and trim and fit as always, he looked pretty intimidating. As soon as the guy snipped the chain, Tim was barking orders again. "Now get in the van and lie down on your stomach." Tim was waving the gun around, using it to point.

"Do you mind pointing that back at him, please?" Hoyt said.

Tim apologized and continued. "Check the tool box for zip ties."

The driver chimed in. "The zip ties . . . on the top shelf. Just don't shoot me! I have kids."

Hoyt scanned the shelf and quickly found a big bag full of heavy-duty eighteen-inch cable ties. He added to the conversation. "You buy these in bulk? You must tie up lots of people." Hoyt zip-tied the driver's hands tightly behind his back and his feet together; not gently, either, not after his days of being locked up like a dog on a leash. He secured the man's belt to the shelf and gave him some last-minute advice as he prepared to slide the side door shut. "Don't forget about those kids of yours. No need to be a hero."

\* \* \*

Inside the house, Lisa was counting down from ten. She had hoped both men would go up into the attic. She knew she had to react before Daz realized she wasn't up there and came back down the ladder. She stuck the Taser against the seat above her, closed her eyes and pushed with all her might. The Taser worked perfectly, even through the wicker, sending Carlos screaming. He sprang up off the bench but fell back onto it, getting Tased again. He fell off the bench, screaming and convulsing, as Lisa struggled to get out of the wicker bench. She quickly flipped over the table full of nails, knocked over the ladder and then pushed the table a couple more feet, lining it up right under the ceiling hole. Flipping the table over sent Carlos' gun clattering to the floor and sliding into the dining area. Carlos was still stunned from the Tasing but recovering quickly. He lay between her and the front door. She tried to step over him, but he grabbed her ankle. She spun around wildly, slicing his bicep with her modified scissors. When he let go, she jammed the Taser into his lower back. This third time, she Tased the shit out of him. Literally. The combination of laxatives Hoyt had tricked him into taking and the third jolt of voltage to his nervous system was enough to make him shit his pants. He'd have to wait to realize how badly he'd been humiliated, though. Carlos had passed out.

Now for Daz, who had appeared in the ceiling hatch. Lisa looked up at him, then both looked down at the table below, bristling with spikes. What would ordinarily have been an easy drop didn't look so easy now. He wouldn't be going anywhere.

Lisa dashed for the front door, Taser in hand, and was startled by Hoyt and Tim as she opened the door. She crouched, Taser at the ready. Tim stepped back defensively and then directed her to Hoyt with his free hand as he scanned the room, pistol pointed in whatever direction he was looking. *Damn*, she thought as she took in Hoyt's condition. *Hoyt looks mighty rough.* Of course, she admitted, with her Taser pointing at them, she probably looked pretty wild-eyed, too. Hoyt laughed, taking in the view of the two subdued men, one up and one down. "Look at you two. Goddamn Bonnie and Clyde."

\* \* \*

Hoyt straddled Carlos' back and zip-tied his hands. His eyes popped open and he struggled for a moment like a subdued alligator. Blood was oozing from the slice on his arm. When he stopped squirming, Hoyt couldn't help repeating a line that Carlos had said to him only two days earlier. "Damn, boy, you stink."

The wail of an approaching siren made Hoyt look up. He saw Tim pointing his gun at the man in the attic. "You got a weapon?" Tim demanded.

The man shook his head. "Nope, Little Miss Pretty down there pretty much kicked our ass."

That made Hoyt laugh again, and repeat his line: "Yeah, Goddamn Bonnie and Clyde."

Lisa pocketed her Taser and ran into Hoyt's arms. Tim backed up to the wall and slid down to a squat, still keeping his gun on the man in the attic. "I can't believe we did it," he said.

The siren got louder and then stopped as a police car pulled up the driveway. Red and blue lights flickered, lighting up the yard and the house. Sergeant Jenkins was accompanied by the precinct's rookie, the kid everyone called "Richie Rich." They entered the house with guns drawn. As Sergeant Jenkins looked around, a grin spread over his face as he confirmed that things were under control. He holstered his gun. "Tim, looks like you've been busy. Maybe you want a job on my force."

The rookie still had his gun out. "Who's that up in the attic?"

Tim stood up, lazily lowering his gun to his side. "That's one of the bad guys, officer."

Richie Rich—Officer Prissue—kept his gun pointed at the guy up in the attic as he addressed Tim. "I'm gonna need that gun, cowboy."

Tim extended his arm, holding the gun's handle with only his thumb and forefinger.

The officer took the gun and tucked his own back into his holster. He pointed Tim's gun back at the man in the ceiling and began to speak. "Let me tell you what just happened here tonight." All eyes went to officer Prissue as he took his aim off the man in the attic and zeroed in on Sergeant Jenkins.

"Prissue, are you crazy? Put the gun down."

Prissue continued. "Tim over here is what we call a loose cannon. You really fucked things up, Tim. I was willing to pay ten million bucks to these bozos for The Gift. Now I can deal directly with you. But I got to be able to trust you. If we can all agree that the guy up in the attic shot Sergeant Jenkins with this gun before I returned fire with my gun and shot him, we can try this arrangement again: my way. I will be glad to shoot anyone not in agreement. Anyone not on board?" Officer Prissue waited a few seconds and continued. "Good." He aimed the gun right between Sergeant Jenkins' eyes and pulled the trigger.

\* \* \*

Tim knew the gun was empty and was ready, waiting for his opportunity to charge the officer. The moment he heard the hammer click he made his move, knocking Prissue into the wall. Jenkins joined in and quickly subdued the rookie cop.

"Bad move, Richie Rich," Jenkins grunted as he slapped the cuffs onto yet another of his supposed teammates. He radioed in, "Adams and Labont, I need you guys here at the Pendleton house ASAP. Tell Guble to bring Lieutenant Jablouski. We're going to need two more squad cars."

Jenkins kept the three men at gunpoint while Tim and Hoyt went out to the van to bring in the driver. In an attempt to free himself, he had pulled the van's shelving down on top of himself. Tim and Hoyt righted the shelf, snipping the zip tie that secured the man to it. They escorted the driver inside and sat him on the floor next to the newly revived Carlos, Daz and the rookie Officer Prissue.

Officer Prissue began muttering under his breath but quickly turned up the volume. "Now you got nothin'." He lifted his head and raised his voice. "You could have walked away with ten million bucks."

Hoyt subtly shook his head. "You were never going to let me live. I heard Carlos tell his boys he was going to bring Lisa to the shed so we could die together."

Officer Prissue was seated right next to Carlos. Their eyes met and Prissue mimed the silent question: asking Carlos if that was true.

Carlos shrugged his shoulders as if to say, "So what if I did?" Despite being handcuffed, Prissue took the opportunity to head-butt Carlos. "Get him away from me. He stinks."

Sergeant Jenkins shook his head and let out a one-syllable laugh. "Hah. You're both idiots." Carlos leaned away from Prissue, causing a chain reaction of movement from Daz and the van driver.

The other officers quickly showed up and escorted the four men outside. Jenkins settled a short argument over who had to transport the humbled and smelly Carlos. "Guble, Jablouski: He goes with you. Adams and Labont, you take these two idiots." He pointed to Daz and his nameless accessory from the van. "I want Prissue in my car. He and I have some catching up to do." As the last head was tucked into the back of the three police vehicles, Jenkins looked back at Hoyt, Lisa and Tim. "You guys are brave. This could have gone way worse. I'll be contacting you for statements once we get this under control." He gave them a nod of approval and eased himself into his car. He gave a double blast on the siren and moments later they were all gone.

Standing together by the front door, Hoyt and Lisa were holding hands. Tim ran both his hands through his hair and rested them on the back of his neck. He tilted his head left and right, obviously tense, before finally breaking the silence. "Wow. Somebody wanna tell me what the hell just happened?"

Hoyt spoke up. "Yeah, I'll tell you what just happened. My badass wife and my gangster best friend just saved my ass." Hoyt hesitated and reached into his pocket, pulling out two tiny earbuds. "He offered us ten million dollars for these little guys. I told you I was on to something."

Lisa shook her head. "Carlos offered us all millions, but all we were ever really going to get from him was a bullet in the head."

The smile fell from Hoyt's face and the dice-size earbuds went back into his pocket.

Lisa went into the house and started putting things back into place. "Tim, help me turn this table right side up." Once the ruined, table was back where it belonged, Tim and Lisa both plopped down, exhausted, on either side. Tim ran his fingers over the pattern of nail heads and gave Lisa an admiring glance.

Hoyt started up again. "I've spent the last three years developing this technology. This could change lives."

Lisa and Tim were silent. Once Hoyt got started, he was perfectly capable of carrying a conversation all by himself. "I could work with doctors, Alzheimer's patients. I could stop premature senility." The earbuds came out of his pocket again and he rattled them around in his palm like he was about to shoot dice. "Lisa . . . We could retire and move to France or Spain . . . Hell, we could do both." Now Lisa was staring down at the nail heads in the table, touching one after another. "We could . . . We could . . . Ahh, shit." Hoyt finally stopped talking and rolled the earbuds across the table.

Now it was Lisa's turn to talk. "Hoyt, I have put up with your obsessive behavior for a long time now. Right now, I just want to get the house back in order and take a shower. And by the way . . . Damn. You stink. So, at least for right now Hoyt, please, I don't want to hear any more about this so-called 'Gift.'" She made air quotes with her fingers.

Tim, Hoyt was grateful to see, was smart enough to stay out of this conversation. "I have to go. My dog is probably freaked out and starving."

Hoyt opened his arms, wafting his three-day-old body odor in Tim's direction, silently asking for a hug from his longtime friend.

Tim responded by offering a fist bump while pinching his nose. Hoyt couldn't help laughing at this.

As Tim stepped through the door, Hoyt pointed at him and muttered, "Cards this Thursday?" He hesitated with a look toward Lisa. "Here at our place."

Tim just smiled and closed the door.

Lisa held out her hand and smiled softly. "C'mon, let's take a shower and climb into bed." As Hoyt walked past the table, he scooped up his two earbuds. He noticed the busted coffee table and flashed back to the night of the abduction for just a moment. He excused himself into the hall bathroom. He took a long moment at the mirror noticing his rough-looking facial growth and then to admire his fit upper body. He flexed momentarily, catching a whiff of his ripe armpits. He peeled off his filthy pants, struggling just a bit because one hand was still grasping what had become known as The Gift. He pushed the tiny earbuds deep into his ears and began speaking a mantra to the man in the mirror. "You are smart. You are sexy. You are a great lover." He smiled at the man in the mirror, closed in to meet him face to face, and continued in a whisper. "Don't ever forget that."

He pulled out the earbuds and stared at them, jiggling them in his hand. Then he dropped them, one at a time, into the toilet and flushed.

### The End ###

Thank you for reading my book. If you enjoyed it, won't you please take a moment to leave a review at your favorite retailer?

## About the Author:

Rick grew up in the Midwest in a big family, so it was easy to get lost in a crowd. According to his brothers, he had an uncanny ability to disappear. He was admittedly reckless as a young man. Any one of a number of his adventures might have resulted in an untimely death.

He'd jump from perfectly good airplanes, swim with alligators or dive in shark infested waters. I asked Rick what scares him most. He replied, "A man with nothing to lose." He hesitated and continued, "Or a sexy woman dressed to the nines. Both are unpredictable."

Other Titles by Rick Incorvia:

*In Your Dreams*

*When I'm Gone*

*Reckless Ambition*

*The Traveler's Best Seller*

Take a sneak peek at *Reckless Ambition* and *In Your Dreams* ...

# Reckless Ambition

*Rick Incorvia*

## Chapter 1 - Meet Rick Timber

The diver surfaced and gave the thumbs up to the sheriff, and then motioned for the crane operator to hoist away. The sunken car had gone unnoticed for three days due to heavy rains. The sun finally came out to reveal the silver hood of an older model car. As the car was slowly lifted from the creek, water oozed from the broken front windshield. A small crowd had gathered. The car belonged to Rick Timber.

Rick had spent the last few years drifting from town to town. He lived with the kind of reckless abandonment that only someone with nothing to lose can. He was brought up in a small rural town in northern Ohio, but he never stayed at any one place very long. By the age of 14 he had been in and out of the detention home. The neighborhood kids knew to steer clear of him.

Barely 24, Rick was living out of a 12-year-old silver Toyota Corolla with a crack in the windshield that seemed to get worse by the day. It was mid-September, and Rick knew he only had a few months of warm weather left before he would need to find some place other than his car to stay. The little clothing he had was in the backseat, wrinkled and smelly. A new stain or tear always seemed to show up. He tried so hard to keep from looking like a bum. He was smart enough to know people judged him by his appearance.

Early one cold morning, he decided to do some clothes shopping at a small local mall. He stopped in the men's room on the way in to tuck in his shirt and slick back his hair with his trusty black comb. He gave his armpits a sniff and decided deodorant would be a nice addition to his glove box. He quietly walked into one of the mall's more casual clothing stores. He was greeted with a smile and a "Good morning."

He squeaked out a crooked smile and continued to the back of the store. He quickly picked out an armful of T-shirts and a pullover shirt with a collar, and hid them under a couple of hooded sweatshirts. As he headed for the dressing room, he was greeted once again by an overzealous employee, "How many items, sir?" He noticed the sign that said, "Max of 4 Items in Dressing Rooms" and quickly snapped, "Four." She trustingly handed him a card with the number four on it and pointed him in the direction of the men's dressing room.

Once inside a tightly closed changing stall, he quickly began layering clothing and finished by putting on one of the hooded sweatshirts. All this took about two minutes, but to give the illusion of authenticity, he wasted an extra few minutes pulling up his socks and tightening the laces on his shoes. As he left, he handed two T-shirts and one of the sweatshirts to the attendant. "If it's OK, I'll just wear this one home." He tore the tag off right in front of the attendant and headed for the cashier.

With two new T-shirts, a new golf shirt, and new sweatshirt, he calmly walked out of sight the attendant and then right past the cashier. He expected to hear the friendly greeter's voice say, "Sir, you pay at the cash register." He had just enough for the sweatshirt, but the cashier was preoccupied so he just kept walking.

Throughout the rest of that day, he wandered in and out of other stores, adding sunglasses, new shoes, and a belt to his collection. Rick didn't have a sense of style. He just tried to blend in and stay warm. He used to get hand-me-downs from his older brother, Andy, but they had drifted apart to say the least.

Rick was nearly 6 feet tall and had jet black hair down to his shoulders. He was about 185 pounds with a modest build. He was handy and was known to convince folks to let him do odd jobs for quick money. He would trim trees or paint garages. He had even built a few nice decks in the neighborhood.

His greasy hair and a scar on his neck seemed to make people nervous. He could always tell when someone was noticing his hair or sneaking a look at his scar. The scar was from an escape gone bad. While running from the scene of one of his petty snatch and runs as a 12- year-old boy, he sliced his neck on an old chicken wire fence while trying to outrun the cops through his neighborhood. He nearly bled to death. This was the incident that put him into the detention home for the first time. The police warned his mother then that this boy was going to be trouble.

Feeling pretty good about his successful shopping spree, he decided to visit his aunt who lived in the area. Aunt Maggie was his mother's sister, but they hadn't spoken in years. They used to visit a lot when Rick was young. Rick's mother was the baby of the family and Maggie always looked after her, at least until the accident.

Aunt Maggie became a widow nearly ten years ago when her husband didn't survive the car accident that nearly took her as well. After the accident, everything changed. Aunt Maggie stayed in the hospital for three months. Along with internal injuries, she broke her hip and lost most of the vision in her right eye. Ten years later, she still walked with an awkward limp but refused to use a cane. Her dark hair was long, but no one knew how long since she always had it wrapped tightly in a bun.

Maggie opened the door just enough to look out with her good eye. Rick greeted her with a big smile and a "Surprise!" She didn't recognize the young man.

"It's me, Aunt Maggie . . . Rick Timber."

A sad smile came to her wrinkly, overweight face as she continued to open the door. She missed her little sister. Maggie was a big part of Rick's life until the age of 12. She remembered he was into mischief as a youngster, but he looked like such a well-mannered young man tonight.

Rick pretended that he was just there for a visit, but he had no intention of leaving that night. He was after a hot shower and a warm bed. He told his aunt that he recently landed a job at the local mall and just had to see how she was doing. Maggie was thrilled to have such young, vibrant company. There were leftovers on the stove, and Rick was quick to praise the wonderful smell coming from the kitchen. Naturally, Aunt Maggie made him up a plate.

It wasn't long before their idle chitchat veered in the direction of her sister. "How is my baby sister?" asked Maggie with a sorrowful face.

Rick went into an elaborate story about a garden she had planted in the backyard. He told tales of tomatoes the size of softballs and corn stalks seven feet tall with ears of corn so big they had to break them in half to fit them into the pot.

In reality, Rick had not seen his mother in two years. Rick attempted to wrap up the conversation about his mother by saying she was working two jobs now and he didn't get to see her much.

"And how about your brother Andy?"

The room fell silent. Andy had been looking for him for two years. Rick had impersonated Andy and sold his precious 1958 two-door Buick Special. Andy was in love with that car. From the dusty streets of Portland, Oregon, to the potholed streets of Cleveland, Ohio, Andy had literally driven that car cross-country. He had spent summer after summer working on his pride and joy until it was fully restored. Short on money, Rick put an ad in the local paper and met the buyer at the storage garage Andy rented. Underselling the car by several thousand, Rick took $6,500.00 for the car nearly two years ago and went into hiding.

Andy was a bigger and stronger version of Rick physically, but nothing like Rick. He was 6' 3" tall and weighed well over 230 pounds. Although he could pass for a boxer or a big-time wrestler, he was the executive type. He was in his late twenties and already a big shot for a fitness franchise, running one of their regional offices.

The thought of running into Andy was frightening. Rick had heard stories from the neighborhood that Andy was looking for him. Andy had a temper like their father.

Realizing his aunt was still waiting for an answer, Rick looked down at the ground and whispered, "I haven't heard from him in years. He's doing good at work. He moves a lot with his job."

Maggie could see this was an awkward subject for Rick and attempted to move on. "So, tell me where you live!"

Again, Rick stuttered as he made up another lie. "I'm in the bad part of town . . . for now," he blurted in an attempt to buy himself more time to think. "I'm about 10 miles straight up Anderson Street and then about 3 more miles north by that old deli."

Aunt Maggie looked puzzled, and again, silence filled the room.

"It's a one bedroom. I haven't unpacked yet so it's mostly just boxes. I haven't even set up my bed yet."

Against her better judgment, and feeling a little obligatory pressure, Aunt Maggie made the offer that Rick was fishing for. "Do you want to stay here tonight? You would have to sleep on the couch."

Maggie was used to being alone. She had a routine. Watch a little TV with her long-haired orange-and-white cat "Scratches" and then read a book while taking a late evening bath to help her fall asleep. With Rick on the couch, there would be no TV, but she could still read her book in the bath.

"Wow, that would be great! All I need is a pillow and a blanket. I'll probably be gone when you wake up, Aunt Maggie. Do you mind if I take a shower in the morning?"

Maggie disappeared for a few minutes and returned with a pillow, a blanket, and an old photo album. She watched as Rick leafed through the dusty, yellowing Polaroid photos. He hesitated at a photo of his mother. He wiped away the dust to get a better look at her and then continued. He forced a smile in Aunt Maggie's direction that quickly drooped to a frown. Rick forced it back to a fake smile and yawned, signaling that he had enough for the night.

Maggie excused herself to straighten up in the kitchen and then returned, turning off lights and mumbling her thoughts out loud. "Good night, Ricky," she said in a voice that made Rick feel like he was 12 again as she headed down the hallway to her room.

He set his $12.00 watch for 4:00 a.m. and quickly fell into a deep sleep. It had been a long time since he slept anywhere other than his car. Maggie was still wound up from the change of routine and the excitement of a visitor. She tossed and turned well into the night.

Rick's timid little watch alarm went off as scheduled. He didn't really need the watch. He was an early riser. Something about watching the sun rise gave him hope. When the tip of the sun first appeared he said aloud, "Today is a new day." He knew he had done his brother wrong. He had a couple of really bad years and made his share of enemies. One day, he planned to make it right again.

He helped himself to a nice hot shower in Aunt Maggie's fancy guest bathroom. She had a huge bottle of shampoo and a small, almost-empty bottle of conditioner. Rick filled the nearly empty conditioner bottle with shampoo, figuring Aunt Maggie would never miss it. That was one less thing he'd have to steal from the store.

He took a good look around the house and decided not to burn this bridge. He could use some family and a warm place to sleep now and then, more than he needed some old lady jewelry or the small amount of cash she might have in her purse. He did take one fork, one spoon, and one knife. Scratches followed him like a mute spy, noting his every move. He figured he would get good use out of the silverware, and she would never miss them.

As he headed for the door, he noticed an envelope taped to the door with his name on it. Inside was a picture of him and his brother standing in front of their mom and dad. He looked to be about four years old. Aunt Maggie had also put a $20 bill in the envelope, along with a small note that said, "Today's a new day." Rick quietly laid the silverware back in the sink, stuffed the picture and the $20 in his back pocket, and went on his way.

The car ignition churned slowly, as if it was too tired to start. Finally, it squealed rudely and ignited into a high-revolution whine. Rick slammed the gas pedal all the way to the floor and quickly released it. The engine eased up as if it recognized Rick as the one who startled him. As he backed out of the driveway, one of the voices in his head woke up. Rick had a name for this person in his head. He called him Egor. He was the keeper of Rick's darker thoughts.

"Why didn't you take anything? We need money to survive, and $20 isn't enough."

Rick dismissed Egor's complaining. He felt so refreshed after a good night's sleep and a hot shower.

Rick thought to himself, "Today is a new day. Maybe it's time for a change. Maybe I should really get a job like everyone else."

Egor overheard and was quick to chime in "Yes, how about Walmart? It would certainly be easier to steal the things we need if we worked there."

It was 5:45 a.m. Rick had his new clean clothes on and was just out of the shower. He parked near the back of the parking lot as he always did. Parking in the back allowed for a quick getaway out the front and a stealthy return from the rear later.

He strolled into the Walmart. It was pretty much deserted this time of day except for the people stocking the shelves. He noticed one of the two cashiers counting down her drawer in anticipation of the end of her shift. He instinctively headed toward her, wondering just how much money was in her drawer and where it must all end up. Egor purposely interrupted her counting, hoping to create an opportunity to separate her from the money. "Excuse me, would I be able to get an application?"

She looked up and gave him a smile, with one index finger up letting him know that she was still counting money and he would have to wait. Instinctively, he began to notice everything about her. The yellow name tag on her Walmart apron with the smiley face said Kim. She had a small diamond nose ring and thick, shiny blond hair. It was shoulder length on the sides and progressively shorter in the back. Her earrings were small silver lightning bolts, and her teeth looked like they just came out of braces. Her smile was perfect. Rick guessed her to be about his age.

She flipped her hand over and used the same finger she used to stop Rick in his tracks to motion for him to follow her. She was just over 5 feet tall and probably 140 pounds of curvy pleasure. She had large breasts trapped in a tight button-up blouse, trying to push their way out of the sides of her apron. Her skin was perfect, and her lips were big and beautiful. She tilted her head upward, silently asking Rick, "What can I do for you?"

Rick responded in a soft, low voice. "I'd like to work here." She looked him up and down and raised an eyebrow that suggested a hint of flirtation.

"Watz ur name, handsome?" she seemed to say all as one word. Her voice was higher than Rick expected, and her walk was slow and confident. He instinctively considered lying about his name but, "Rick. Rick Timber" slipped out without warning.

She smiled and motioned with her seductive eyes for him to grab a seat while she temporarily put her money drawer under a counter. When she bent over, her breasts nearly fell out of her top. She watched as Rick's eyes dropped to her blouse and smiled. "My eyes are up here sweetheart."

Rick blushed while Egor's thoughts were on the cash. "I wonder how much money is in that drawer." Rick tuned out the untimely voice in his head. Kim held out an application for Rick but kept hold of it as he attempted to take it from her.

"Can you work nights, Mr. Timber?" she asked, still keeping hold of the application, forcing him to look right into her blue eyes.

"Sure . . . I'm new to the area and—"

"Great," she said interrupting him. "You can start tomorrow. Well, it would actually be tonight," she clarified. "I will train you myself. Be here at 11:00 p.m." Rick let go of the application. Apparently, the interview was over.

With the rest of the day ahead of him and a new job in the bag, Rick decided to enjoy the day. He had almost a 1/2 tank of gas and twenty more dollars, thanks to Aunt Maggie.

He drove to a busy little boardwalk only minutes from Walmart, where there were sure to be valuables for the taking for anyone with a little patience and a lot of nerve. Egor was hard to suppress at times like this.

Things were quiet for the first 20 minutes, and Rick kept thinking about how Kim held on to the application and made him look her in the eyes. Was this his opportunity to go straight and live a normal life, earning a steady paycheck, or was this just another opportunity for Egor to take from the rich and give to himself?

His concentration was broken when two elderly ladies clumsily ordered ice cream from the walk-up ice cream vendor. Egor was awake and watching with an eagle eye, waiting for an opportunity to separate one of them from their purse. It was no use. These gals were veterans, and they clung to their purses like fullbacks holding a football.

Almost an hour later, a young businessman set his laptop and cell phone on a table in a fairly busy outdoor common dining area. He placed his briefcase on the ground by his chair. He took a quick look around and decided his belongings would be safe since he would have them in sight at all times. He headed only 20 feet away to get himself a Philly Steak sandwich. Egor told Rick to wait. He knew the man would look back one more time before he ordered. The businessman got to the front of the line and, like clockwork, looked over his shoulder to make sure no one was messing with his stuff.

The moment he started to order, Rick walked up to the table, sat down, and began tapping on the laptop keys as if it were his. He calmly picked up the cell phone and began to fake a conversation. Moments into the conversation, he closed up the laptop, placed it in the briefcase, and vanished into the crowd.

Rick was no stranger at the local pawnshops. He knew there was one on Anderson Street, only three miles from the boardwalk. Larry ran a tight ship. This was the kind of place that you had to stand at the front door while waiting to get buzzed in and the door would lock behind you.

The locals had been trying to force Larry out of business with legislation for years, and yet he thrived. He knew most of Rick's stuff was stolen and usually only offered him ten cents on the dollar. That laptop was good for a quick $60.00, and Rick looked forward to a full tank of gas, a full belly, and some money in his pocket.

It wasn't until 4:00 p.m. that he once again remembered about his strange "interview" and that he had a job to go to at 11:00 p.m. that night. He found a remote spot in the parking lot of a Holiday Inn. His parking spot came with a water view. He had a dozen favorite parking spots around town. He chose them carefully. They had to offer something special . . . a beautiful sunrise or sunset, a sky full of stars, or a stakeout with promise of prosperity.

He watched the sun set as he reflected on the day's events, and right on cue, Egor started in on him. "Nice job with the laptop today, that was smooth. You know you could have gotten $300 bucks or more for that if you had a little more patience. You better be careful with this Kim chick at Walmart. There is something strange about her."

Rick didn't feel like arguing tonight. It had been too good of a day. He set his trusty watch alarm for 10:00 p.m. and dozed off. He was all too used to sleeping in his car.

Rick was rudely awakened by bright headlights as a mid-sized mobile home slowed to a crawl, looking for a quiet place to park for the night. Rick watched as the mobile home went by. He always dreamed of owning one of his own.

It was 9:15 p.m. and Rick decided to get a bite to eat before starting his new job. He drove back down Anderson Street looking for a place to sit and eat. He kept thinking of Kim and her big breasts. Egor was coaching him, "Don't take a stupid stock job or cleanup deal. You need to be running a register."

Rick noticed a Red Lobster, and Egor seemed to grab the steering wheel and turn the car in. As always, Rick parked in the back. He walked in, and immediately Egor began to case the joint, noticing where the cash register was located and what buttons the cashier pushed to get the register to open. Rick had to remind Egor to relax and enjoy a meal.

The Red Lobster greeter was busy organizing the area, stacking scattered menus and returning crayons to their bucket. Rick let her fuss while he took in the view and layout of the restaurant. He spotted a well-dressed couple in a fairly remote area of the restaurant. He figured this would be a quiet area to gather his thoughts. He strategically sat so he could take in the view of the well-dressed woman with long dark hair and cleavage worthy of being caught staring. He kept a booth between them so his intentions would not seem too obvious.

She was talking endlessly in a soft voice while her male friend silently continued to feed his face. His back was to Rick, but he could see this was a pretty good-sized man just by the way he filled out his suit.

The sound of his fork scraping the plate to organize the food into bigger bites was instantly annoying to Rick. He working that plate like a machine clearing a field of debris.

Rick was greeted by a husky waitress named Betty. He quickly opened the dinner special insert that was tucked into the menu and pointed to the daily special. She made her notes and asked what he wanted to drink. He tapped his coffee cup, and his order was completed without a word being spoken.

A moment or two later, the woman with the low-cut dress got up to use the restroom. She was stunning. Her dress had a beautiful red and white pattern and a slit way up the one side, revealing one of her long, silky legs. Her breasts bounced as she walked by, and Rick couldn't take his eyes off her. She expected nothing less and gave him a smile that went right to the brain in his pants. Egor sized her up to be 5' 9" and about 120 pounds. Most of the 20 pounds were full and flawless bouncing boobs. From behind, Rick could see the elbow of the big man was still shoveling in his meal. His head was inches from his plate, and the fork was working overtime like a steam shovel. The smell of food in the restaurant had Rick anticipating his hot meal, and he took in a deep breath and exhaled a moan of delight.

He was used to eating cold food. His diet consisted of eating the food that he placed into a shopping cart while pretending to grocery shop. He had to eat items that would quickly disappear from a shopping cart to his mouth. His favorite items were grapes, small candy bars, peanuts, lunch meats of all kinds, and Pringles chips. He would slowly fill a cart while leisurely shopping, pretending to read labels and munching on the things in his cart. The event might take over an hour. When he was full, he would simply abandon his cart.

Rick heard footsteps and could not wait to see this woman return, this time giving him the pleasure of seeing her from behind. The footsteps unfortunately belonged to Betty, his manly waitress. She clumsily plopped down a plate full of Shrimp Scampi with steamed vegetables and a pot of coffee.

Rick was starving and began to dig right in. Egor told him to slow down. "You're eating like the guy two booths down." Again, the sound of footsteps approached. This time, he knew it was her. The click of her shoes instantly flashed Rick back to five minutes ago. He closed his eyes and was able to relive her slow, seductive walk with that tight dress showing off her perfect curves.

He pretended not to notice, but everything went into slow motion as she walked by. She had a skinny waist and a round ass that banged so nicely from side to side with every step. Egor was deep into Rick's head, whispering all kinds of sexual comments about what he would like to do with her. When she got to her booth, she turned and looked right at Rick again. He was frozen as she hiked her dress just enough to get back into the booth . . . just enough to once again force Rick's eyes toward her forbidden zones.

The man with her called her by name, "Melissa, do you see our waitress? We have to go."

Rick's heart began to pound heavily. His brain went from sexual to survival in an instant. That voice was all too familiar. It was Andy. He would surely beat the tar out of him right here in the restaurant until the police arrived. The police were no friend of Rick's either. Egor was quick to take control of the situation. "What are you waiting for? Go now before he notices you."

Rick looked at the meal he wouldn't be able to finish. He took one last bite and a gulp of his coffee, and stood up quietly, hoping to slip out unnoticed. As he stood up, Egor could not help giving Melissa a subtle wink and a smile. She smiled back, and Andy struggled to turn his big body to see who she was flirting with. Rick's new stolen sweatshirt with the hood instantly became his favorite piece of clothing.

"Who was that?" Andy blurted in his don't-fuck-with-me voice. Melissa quickly responded, "Just a young teenager I caught staring at me."

Melissa was always looking for attention from men and loved to get Andy jealous. If she played her cards right, she got gifts from him to remind her why she was with him. If she overplayed the moment, somebody was getting a beating.

She was well aware of Andy's temper. Just last week while at a nice martini bar, Melissa took her flirting just a bit too far with a young curly haired buck, and Andy exploded without warning.

He walked up to the man only inches away from his face and looked right into his eyes. Andy embedded his huge right hand into the back of the man's thick, curly locks and began tightening his grip and analyzing his model-like facial features. With one quick motion, he smashed his head into the bar, instantly breaking his nose. The man lifted his bloody face just in time to greet Andy's huge left fist. The barrage of hammering blows to the head and chest quickly put the man to the ground, knocking down chairs, rearranging tables, and spilling drinks. The man lay on his back, unable to put a coherent thought together. Andy lifted the nearly unconscious man horizontally nearly a foot from the ground by his torn and now-bloodied button-up shirt and started with a verbal assault. Melissa had her hands over her face, just hoping it would end soon.

It took three men to pull Andy off of him. He ripped free from their grasp and looked at them as if to say, "I'm done with him, you wanna be next?"

The biggest guy put his hands in the air defensively and said, "Man, you need to calm down."

Andy straightened his shirt and ran both his hands through his hair from front to back as he slowly began to regain his composure. As the attention moved to the moaning man on the ground, Andy grabbed Melissa firmly by the arm. "Are you happy now? Is that what you wanted? Let's go." Beauty and the beast disappeared out the door.

The time was now 10:30, and Rick decided to forget about eating and head to Walmart to see about his new job and Kim. Egor kept talking about Melissa. "Did you see the curves on her? I don't think she was wearing anything under that dress."

All Rick was concerned about was why Andy was in this part of town. Was it just a coincidence or did he live in the area now? He was often transferred to a troubled fitness location to help get things back in order. He looked 20 pounds heavier . . . all muscle. He would surely turn Rick in to the police after giving him a good brotherly beating for the Buick incident.

As he entered the store, he looked for Kim at the register where they met only 17 hours earlier. Two new faces were at the registers, and Egor began to nag, "Maybe this isn't a good idea . . . Let's just pick up some things we need and get the hell out of here."

Just then, Kim poked him from behind and said, "Good, you came back," and again the forefinger wiggled the familiar sign for follow me.

Rick followed her into an area that customers don't get to see. There were tables and chairs and vending machines and even Rick's sworn enemy, the time clock. Kim dropped an array of forms in front of him. On top was the application she was so reluctant to give up much earlier this morning. Rick looked at the stack of papers and then back at Kim. "Can we do this after the shift?"

Kim looked at him and told him to fill out the application now, insinuating that the rest of the paperwork could wait. Rick filled out his real name since he told her it last night. Egor convinced him to spell it Rick Timburr instead of Rick Timber, and everything else on the application was a flat-out lie. He used his aunt's street and a made-up address. He made up his last two jobs to be at grocery stores and claimed to be trained as a cashier. He acquired two years of community college just by writing it down.

After ten minutes, he confidently raised his application toward Kim who was busy adjusting her apron to show off her cleavage and securing her name tag over the stain on her apron. She took his application and handed him an apron of his own and a blank name tag. Rick asked if he could use a nickname on his name tag.

"What ya have in mind?" she asked with a raised and heavily plucked eyebrow. He had no idea but knew that he didn't want to put his real name on that stupid name tag.

"Sometimes I go by Egor" slipped out of his mouth compliments of Egor.

Kim looked at him with curious crystal blue eyes. She took the name tag from him and said, "Egor it is," as she wrote the name much too large for Rick's liking on the name tag. As Kim read over his application, Rick reluctantly put on his new monkey suit with his alter ego pinned to his chest. "Good, ya have register experience," she mumbled from behind her big, kissable lips. "I'll work with ya until ya feel confident enough to work on yer own."

That was the most Kim had ever said at one time, revealing her southern accent. Rick was confident he would master the register quickly with a little help from his mental companion, Egor. Egor watched every move any cashier ever made, in hopes of someday being in a position to rescue abandoned money from its register.

In less than an hour, Kim was observing Rick from a distance. It was busier than he expected. He was suddenly aware of every Walmart bleep. At one point, near the end of his shift, Rick had seven customers in line. Kim watched from a distance while he quickly rang them up and sent them on their way.

She adjusted her apron to once again accent her impressive cleavage and headed for the register. She was intrigued by Rick's confidence. It was almost 6:00 a.m. and Kim still needed to have him fill out paperwork. Quietly sneaking up behind him, she pushed herself against him and whispered in his ear, "Don't take any more customers after the ones in line now so we can take your drawer to the safe." Kim pressed her whole body against him a second time while she reached around him to turn off his register light.

Egor seemed to have a knack for keeping count of how much was in the register. It had to be well over $4,000. With only two customers left in line, another woman tried to enter Rick's line, and he had to tell her he was closing and could not take any more customers.

Moments later, a morning rush of customers made their way to the register area. They were on their toes and twisting their necks to see where the shortest open line was with a cashier. Another couple entered his line. He almost spoke before noticing it was Andy and his not-so-dressed-up girlfriend Melissa. They were third in line.

Eight hours as an honest man, and his life and new job just took a quick turn for the worst. Melissa already had her eyes on him, but Andy was busy looking at the hot women on the magazine covers, meant to keep you from getting bored in line. Rick had to leave now! His heart was racing. He had to remain calm. He quickly scooped up the wad of large bills stashed under the drawer and all the twenties from the register and quietly told the next customer in line that he needed to get change and would be right back. He professionally organized and tucked the bills into his apron pocket and simply said, "Excuse me."

Then he did what he did best. He disappeared into the crowd. As soon as he was in a quiet aisle, he took the money from the apron and stuffed it in his pockets. He tucked the apron and name tag behind some cereal boxes and headed for the front exit, hoping to look like just another customer.

He knew he was on camera and could not head for the car. When he got out the front door, he pulled up his hood and hoped to pass as a jogger. He jogged steadily for about a half-mile before ducking into a little strip mall. He tried to calm down and decide on his next move. He had to go back for the car, but not yet. He frantically searched the landscape for somewhere to become invisible. He noticed the familiar neon glow of an all-night laundromat across the street. He could wash the now-sweaty clothes while waiting to see how the Walmart incident played out.

He nursed a washing machine, keeping it a secret that all he had in it was one lousy T-shirt. The minutes ticked by slowly as he imagined cop cars swarming the area. When his shirt was done, he took off his favorite hooded sweatshirt and slipped on the warm T-shirt.

He started the wash and dry process all over again, again with only one item of clothing.

Rick spent the next hour working himself into a frenzy. He had to go back for the car, but that was insane; surely Kim could identify him.

"They've probably reviewed my application and the store tapes by now. Kim has no doubt described me in detail to a professional sketcher."

His first thought was to change his clothes and put on a hat, and then he remembered seeing a hair salon at the strip mall.

It was 9:45 a.m. and the strip mall parking lot was quiet except for a few cars in front of the salon. He was unable to tell if the salon was open from the laundromat. He pushed his black hair behind his ears and into his now-clean sweatshirt to make it look shorter. He calmly but quickly walked across the street. He pushed the salon door open just a bit too hard and as it banged against the wall and came to an abrupt stop, all eyes were on Rick. It was definitely a girly salon, complete with hair dryers and old ladies getting their white hair dyed to brown or blue.

"Can I help you, sir?" asked the middle-aged attendant, wondering if he had wandered in by mistake.

"Yes," Rick said and hesitated for a moment. "I am ready for a change," he said as a smile stretched across his face. "I'm ready for a big change."

Rick came out two hours later, waving to his new white-haired friends. They couldn't remember having so much fun with a customer. Rick told them he was tired of the old boring Jim (this time he remembered to lie about his name) and was looking for a whole new identity. They all got involved, even the customers. He had them laughing, asking all of them to put in their two cents for his new look. He told them he was tired of looking like the janitor. He was ready to look like a movie star.

This was hardly the salon to give Rick a Hollywood hairstyle, but he had fun just the same, hanging out with this group of jolly grey-haired grandmothers. The whole time he was there he watched and listened for cops passing by. He was at ease knowing this would be the last place the police would come looking for him.

This band of colors and clippers gave him a whole new look. His hair was short and spiky and lightened to a color they called mocha-something. They even lightened and plucked his thick eyebrows.

Rick walked back toward his car, confident that he was not the same person who was being sought after for grand theft. He was concerned that they may have figured out his real name and somehow had his car under surveillance. He walked past the parking lot once to see if he could tell if his car was being watched. The parking lot was pretty full and people were coming and going. Rick pulled his key out and walked up to the car next to his and pretended to unlock the door. He didn't notice anyone giving him a second look and decided to just get in his car and go.

The car started right up, and Rick quickly slammed the shifter into reverse. As he got to the exit of the parking lot, he hesitated. He had no plan and didn't even know if he should turn left or right. He just knew he couldn't stay. He had no idea of the series of events to follow that would so drastically change his life. He had no way of knowing this chance encounter would be so significant.

*Rick Incorvia*

# In Your Dreams

*Rick Incorvia*

# Chapter 1 - Meet Adam Valentino

The ambulance was closing in fast and Adam was forced to pull to the side of the narrow country road. The berm was steep, so he was careful to pull off only as far as he had to without rolling his car into the icy, water-filled ditch.

In the rearview mirror, Adam was able to see that the huge vehicle was coming fast and the driver was struggling to maintain control in the snow. As the ambulance closed in, the siren became unbearable. Adam inched forward another few feet, and a few more inches off the slippery pavement.

It became obvious that the ambulance wouldn't be able to pass him on the slick road without making some kind of contact. His hands were gripping the steering wheel so tightly that he thought he was going to rip it off. As the deafening rig zipped by him, it tore off his side mirror. The car jolted forward, causing Adam's foot to slip from the brake pedal onto the gas. The car accelerated toward the steep ditch. Adam jammed his foot down with all his might on what he thought was the brake pedal. He was wrong. The engine revved as the tires spun out of control.

He yanked the wheel hard to the left to avoid the

ditch. Everything went into slow motion as the car began to flip over. The ambulance siren was still echoing in his ears, as the car balanced on its right side for a moment. Seconds later, it came crashing down into the murky ditch, splashing upside down into the freezing water.

Adam was lying face down on the floor beside his bed with his covers clenched tightly in his sweaty hands. His alarm clock continued doing its best imitation of a siren. He lay there, unable to move his arms, as if he was still trapped inside the car. If he closed his eyes, the noise of the alarm would send him back to the dream, and back to the ditch. His grip on the covers began to loosen, and control of his limbs slowly returned.

He hated dreams like these. Too many mornings started with a similar nightmarish dream, always of an accident. They were frightening, and so difficult to distinguish from reality. His heart was still pounding a mile a minute as he crawled back onto his bed and reached for his alarm. He held it in both hands for a moment before pressing the OFF button, finally silencing the ambulance.

He looked at the alarm clock with bloodshot eyes. It was 6:01 a.m., and time to start another day. He stumbled into the large kitchen of his luxury home and dropped the alarm into the trash compactor. That was the second alarm to end up in the compactor this month.

He pushed the button on the coffee maker and sat at the kitchen island, content to listen to the coffee brewing. He put his elbows on the granite top and put his head in his hands, staring at an imaginary spot in space, happy to be thinking absolutely nothing.

The phone rang and Adam ignored it for seven rings. Finally, he picked it up. "I'm awake," he mumbled. It was his sister, Julie. She called Adam every morning at 6:10 exactly, to make sure he was awake.

"Were you dreaming again?"

"I always dream, Julie, you know that. I'll call you later," he mumbled, hanging up the phone.

He had no intention of calling back. And he knew Julie didn't believe him. He never called back. Still, she had called him back faithfully every morning since the awful motorcycle accident that had nearly taken his life.

Before the accident, Adam had spent his days negotiating multi-million-dollar real estate deals and entertaining high rollers. By the age of 31, he was a millionaire, often jetting off to Panama for nightlife and Macau for high stakes gambling.

Since the accident, Adam spent most of his time negotiating deals from his laptop. Many of his friends and associates had written him off for dead when the first month went by and he was still in a coma. His recovery was slow and painful, leaving him bitter.

Adam was a handsome man, with a smile and a wit that closed deals. However, his new scar changed the way he saw himself, and therefore, the way others saw him. Today would be like most days, spent tapping away at his laptop from the comforts of the oversized recliner in his living room.

Just before sunset, he sent the final email of the

day to his friend and long-time business partner, Antonio. They had spent the last eight months trying to close a deal on a 12,000 square-foot mansion overlooking the Gulf of Mexico. The $3 million deal was on the brink of falling through, due to the involvement of an unscrupulous lawyer. Antonio had just informed Adam that he was no longer interested in the mansion deal and that he would have to pursue it by himself if he was still interested.

Adam closed the lid to his laptop and slid it into the custom side pocket of his recliner. He thought for a moment, took a deep breath with his eyes closed, and exhaled slowly. He picked up his cell phone and quickly tapped in a number from memory. He cleared his throat as the phone began to ring. A woman answered in a robotic voice, listing the names of the law firm's partners.

"Hello, this is Adam Valentino. I'd like to talk to Mike Viomanda, please."

"I'm sorry, sir; Mr. Viomanda is on vacation until Monday. Would you like to leave him a message?"

Adam felt his blood pressure rising quickly.

"Give him this message: tell him if he doesn't call Adam back on the Gulf mansion by 9 a.m. tomorrow, the deal is off."

He pushed the end button hard. There were a hundred other deals out there he could be pursuing but this one had gotten personal.

Adam was squeezing his phone as he walked into his bedroom to put on a shirt. He tossed his cell phone onto the bed and riffled through the huge selection in his closet. He grabbed a shirt and his keys, and began to dress as he headed for the garage. Tonight, he was going to find a noisy club, slam a few drinks, and attempt to bring home some action.

His drinking had gotten progressively worse over the last few months. Before the accident, Adam considered himself strikingly handsome, but with his new scar, he felt the world owed him something.

Adam cruised down the main drag toward the beach, clicking through commercials on the radio to find some music to put him in a better mood. The low rumble of an accelerating motorcycle interrupted his search. As the bike got closer and louder, Adam felt his hands tighten on the steering wheel. The sound of his own motorcycle zipping through the gears used to make his heart pound with life. Now it brought him back to the day that changed his life.

It wasn't his fault that the SUV driver didn't see him on his fancy new motorcycle. He knew he was going too fast, but he had the right of way. When she turned in front of him, it was already too late for evasive maneuvering. He never even had a chance to hit the brakes. He hit her head-on at 60 miles per hour. As the bike hit her front passenger-side wheel, his head slammed into the bike's windshield, splitting his face wide open. He was lucky enough to land on the hood of the car behind her, rather than being run over by it.

He spent the next 35 days in a coma, unaware that he was in a hospital. In his mind, he continued making big deals and meeting powerful people. While on life support, Adam also created Eva. She was a dark, mysterious woman best described as a black widow. She lived deep in his subconscious. In his dreams, Eva could seduce a man or woman with a glance. Her essence oozed of sensual pleasure. Many words could be used to describe her: attractive, desirable, enticing, erotic, and indulgent. To see her was to want her, and she knew it.

When Adam was with Eva, he was in his dream world. It was in this world that he obsessed over her. Whenever he ran into Eva, he knew he was dreaming. The problem was that Adam preferred Eva to reality. She tormented him with a secret that she seemed to want to share with him. She always took him somewhere exotic, erotic, or just plain strange. She was trying to help him figure out something, but what?

Adam closed the door of his silver Jaguar XJ and walked up the steps of the Crystal Beach Bar. He and his buddies used to strut into this place like they owned it. Since the accident, his buddies had moved on without him.

Once he was settled in at the bar, Adam ordered a vodka martini and casually laid his keys on the bar next to him, making sure that the Jag emblem was visible. He casually stirred his drink with his finger and slipped into thoughts of the pending Gulf mansion deal.

A soft voice broke his concentration. "Are you waiting for someone, or can I join you?"

Adam looked up to see a beautifully bronzed woman. She was turning every head in the bar in a white summer dress that hugged her curves. Adam knew he was still striking from the left side and positioned himself accordingly. He was over six feet tall, well-built, and almost always well-dressed. Even his casual clothes had Italian designer labels. Tonight, however, his shirt was untucked with the collar up and he hadn't shaved in two days.

"Not tonight, sweetheart," he said in his slight European accent. His sleeves were rolled up, showing off his biceps. He usually wore his hair fairly short, but hadn't gone in for a cut in nearly two months. When his hair got this long, he would habitually run his right hand across his head from front to back to get the hair out of his eyes. "I came here to make love to a Stoli martini," he continued as he raised his drink to his lips.

"So did I," she said under her breath as she fingered through her tiny purse on the bar. Her soft white dress exposed both shoulders and hugged her breasts and waist. She was tall and fit and easy to look at. Adam gave her a quick look up and down and continued stirring his drink with his finger. He believed rejection was the best way to get a beautiful woman interested.

She hung her purse on the back of her stool and held up a credit card between her first two fingers. Once she had the bartender's attention, she placed the card on the bar. She slowly eased her tight bottom onto the bar stool next to Adam.

"Two Stoli martinis," she instructed as she pointed to Adam and then back to herself, "and keep 'em comin' on my tab."

Neither of them said a word until the drinks showed up.

"Thank you . . . Miss Beautiful Lady."

"Roanna," she said without looking up from her drink.

"Thank you, Roanna."

Adam sucked down the last of his martini and pushed the empty glass towards the bartender's edge of the bar. He suavely picked up the fresh one Roanna had ordered. He turned to face her eye to eye, exposing his awful scar.

"To God's sense of humor."

Adam expected her to pretend she didn't see the prominent scar. To his surprise, she tenderly grabbed his chin to study the salmon-colored worm embedded in his forehead.

"The scar is pretty cool . . . but your attitude sucks."

This beautiful and mysterious woman kept Adam's strong chin in her hand, carefully studying his scar. She eased up her grip and worked her fingernails under his jaw like she was scratching a dog under the chin.

"And you might consider shaving now and then."

Adam smiled, but he said nothing as he began to take in her features. The white dress looked like it was made of a mix of cotton and spandex, revealing the body of a beach goddess. Her long blond hair fell in loose curls that gently wound their way down to perfectly proportioned breasts. Adam felt a desire to grab her thin waist. Her legs spread apart at the knees as she turned to face him, and she used her free hand to push the fabric of her dress gently down between her thighs. Her legs were strong and flawlessly shaved. Her lacy sandals showed off her sexy, pedicured feet and painted toenails.

Adam extended his right hand palm up, and motioned with his eyes for Roanna to grab it. Roanna looked at his hand and then back into his eyes. She extended her soft left hand slowly, as if preparing to pet a dog that had bitten her in the past. Adam waited patiently until her hand slid deeply into his. She wiggled uncomfortably in her seat, wondering what this stranger was up to. His eyes closed and he slowly let his head drop downward as if he were praying. Roanna watched curiously, but couldn't help looking around the bar to see if anyone else was noticing his strange behavior.

Since the accident, Adam swore he was able to touch people and feel their thoughts. His head slowly lifted, eyes still closed as he pictured Roanna walking along the water's edge with her sandals in her hand.

"Hey, anybody in there?" Roanna asked in a gentle, welcoming voice. Again, she looked around the bar to see if anyone was watching.

Adam whispered, "Yes, I am here. Shhhhhhh."

His accent and impenetrable personality had Roanna feeling uncomfortable but curious for more interaction. He slowly opened his eyes while squeezing her hand and looked right through her.

"I saw you walking alone on a white sandy beach. You had your sandals in one hand, and something small in the other hand. You were sad. You threw something into the water. What was it?"

Roanna's eyes widened as she straightened her posture. "It was a ring."

Adam continued in his soft, arousing voice. "And this ring, it was worth a fortune."

Roanna went silent for a moment. "Not to me . . . not from him."

Over the next ten minutes, the conversation flowed. To an observer, their body language was that of lovers. She adjusted his collar and tucked his hair behind his ear. He stood her up, and held her hand above her head. She instinctively twirled around to let him take in her exemplary body. He put his big hands around the waist he had been admiring and looked into her eyes. She moved in for a kiss but stopped inches from his lips.

"If I let you kiss me. . ." she hesitated.

Adam was slowly closing the gap between their lips. Roanna stopped talking and closed her eyes. His big hands got lost in her blond curls, and his thumbs caressed her ears. When she felt his breath, her lips pushed out in anxious anticipation. Their lips met for a perfect, sultry kiss. Adam tightened his grip on her hair as their martini-soaked lips pushed together harder. When he eased up to back away, Roanna gently brought him back for more. Something about this stranger was making her hot . . . and wet.

Roanna eased him away from her body and sat back on her stool. Her heart was pounding, her head confused by her sudden arousal. She took a long sip of her martini and sensually placed the olive into her mouth. She eyed the bartender and slid her Visa card toward him. She looked back at Adam and whispered into his ear. "Let's go to my house. We can walk there from here."

Roanna lived about a quarter of a mile up the beach. They walked along the waterline with their shoes in their hands. Roanna looked like an angel, with the full moon reflecting off of the non-stop waves. Her windblown hair whipped across her face. Adam had his pants rolled up, but they were still getting wet.

"Do you come to this bar often to seduce men and bring them to your hideaway?"

Roanna smiled and responded, "My last victim is still at the house. Alive, but just barely." She stopped walking and took in Adam's sinfully playful smile; she said nothing, as three consecutive waves washed her calves. Finally, she spoke again. "I haven't dated anyone in years."

Adam seized the moment, putting one hand on Roanna's waist and the other on her neck to pull her in for another kiss. She closed her eyes and let Adam softly kiss and then gently bite her bottom lip. He eased himself back to enjoy her closed-eyed look of desire. Her eyes opened and she began to focus on Adam's face. She moved her thumb across his lips to remove a smudge of lip gloss. She looked at him in a final attempt to try to size him up, either as a player or the real deal. She pulled him in close as if to kiss him. Instead, she backed off and took in his ready-to-kiss face. She gave in to her passion and turned his head to nibble his ear softly as she whispered, "Follow me."

Roanna made her way up three sandy steps and slipped an oversized old key into the lock on a beautiful wrought-iron fence. She slid her fingers between his, and pulled him into the plush pool area of her waterfront playhouse.

Roanna's beach house was magnificent. They had entered through the back beach entrance and stood in an outlandish outdoor Tiki bar area. Her pool area rivaled the beach bar with waterfalls, colored pool lights, and soft luxurious furniture. Adam took the opportunity to soak in the lavish surroundings while Roanna fixed them each another martini at the poolside bar.

She smiled as she handed Adam his drink and held hers out in anticipation of a toast. Adam repeated something he said earlier in the night, but this time with a smile as he nodded his head in approval. "To God's sense of humor."

Without warning, Roanna put her drink down on the bar and began to strip playfully down to her thong. Adam watched intently as she turned and sashayed into the heated pool. He took a long slow sip of his drink and set it back down on the bamboo bar. As he took off his clothes, he couldn't help but wonder if there was a jealous "man of the house" about to blast through the door pointing a pistol at him. Roanna's perfect ass slowly disappearing into the water distracted him from developing the thought further and pulled him toward her like a magnet.

Roanna looked over her shoulder and reached out her arm, signaling Adam to join her in the pool. She turned to admire his naked, masculine body as his hand joined hers. She led Adam to the waterfall and turned to face him. She tilted her head back slightly to let the waterfall rinse her hair. It flowed over her shoulders and her now-erect nipples. She slipped through to the other side, leaving the elegance of the illuminated wall of water to separate them. They held hands through the stream, able to see a distorted version of each other through the falls. Adam slowly walked through the glistening streaming water and they pressed their bodies together, their wet lips sampling each other like candy.

Roanna took one of her hands off of Adam long enough to pull her tiny panties down to her knees. Adam used his toes to pull them down to her ankles. As she stepped completely out of them, Adam picked her up and walked her through the waterfall and up the steps to the pool deck. He gently placed her on one of the round, plush chaise lounges made for two. She could feel the heat coming from his stiff member. He tucked her wet hair behind her ear and began to kiss her neck. She grabbed his firm ass and squeezed, just hard enough to let him know she approved and wanted more. Adam's kisses found their way to Roanna's breasts. His tongue flickered her erect nipples and she arched with anticipation.

Roanna's pool area was only three steps up from the beach and fairly private, but part of its charm was its access to the beach. Anyone passing by on the beach tonight would get a free show.

Suddenly hearing voices from the beach, Roanna decided to take her naked conquest inside. She led Adam through the living room and into the master suite. His trained eyes tried to take in the details of the house, noticing walls made entirely of natural rock and decorative stone. But Roanna's body . . . wow . . . Roanna's body! Her thin waist rolled into a smooth, round ass and her natural, round breasts bounced and swayed gently with every step.

The master bedroom had a huge fireplace and sheer white fabric was draped from the mahogany bed posts. The pool, in all its brilliance, was visible through sparkling glass doors. Waterfalls, colored lights, and gas flame torches brought the pool to life. A romantic Conga beat seemed to be pulsing right through the walls.

Roanna sat on the edge of the bed motioning for him to come closer. Adam stood naked in front of her. She admired his manhood again and he put two fingers under her chin to bring her eyes back to his. She began to speak, but Adam moved his fingers from her chin to her lips, silencing her. He used the same two fingers to gently push her onto her back. He climbed over her sinisterly and moved his fingers across her plump lips. She attempted, but failed, to take them into her mouth. Adam's hands began to investigate her entire body like a child with a new toy. He admired her breasts for a long time, feeling them from every angle and then pinching her nipples ever so gently. He looked up into her eyes and noticed that she was intrigued by his obsession with her body. All ten of his fingers met at her belly button and he began to play with the line of soft blond hair that formed just above and just below her navel. He slid his hands under her waist, pulled her tight, tanned tummy to his lips, and began to kiss her. He began above her tan line, then made his way below. Adam gently began to investigate her erotic zones with his soft touch and talented mouth. Roanna had one hand covering her mouth and the other between her breasts trying to control the pounding of her heart. Adam's soft touch and hot wet kisses quickly brought her to orgasm. Roanna lay on the bed with her hands at her sides, fingers spread apart, palms down on the mattress. Her hands clenched the sheets tightly as she felt Adam begin to enter her. She let out a long, slow moan as he entered her completely.

They made love into the night, stopping only to drink, making one silly toast after another, followed by drunken laughter. A final erotic scene on the bench of the walk-through shower and the oversexed couple was ready to pass out in Roanna's magnificent bed.

The next morning, Roanna woke up first and made coffee. She brought a cup into the bedroom and set it on the nightstand. Adam lay face down, naked without a stitch of covers on him. Roanna smiled sinfully at her hot conquest. She hadn't had sex like that in . . . ever. She took a long sip of her coffee and jumped into the shower, hoping Adam would wake up and join her before she left for a conference in Chicago.

Another hour passed as Roanna dressed up in a beautiful white silk wrap blouse and a gray pencil skirt. Adam still showed no sign of life. Roanna hated the idea of leaving the sexy stranger in her house. She was going to be out of town for three days and was hoping to see this mystery man again . . . and again.

She decided to leave a note on the night stand, thanking him for a wonderful night of romance. In the note, she let him know she would be out of town for a few days, but she would be available by cell phone if he was in need of another attitude adjustment. She took a last look at Adam's muscular ass and fought off the urge to smack it. As a final touch, she left a lipstick kiss on the letter.

*Rick Incorvia*

Made in the USA
Middletown, DE
14 January 2022

58641359R00089